Brodie stared down at the woman in his arms

Her head rested below his chin, her hand lay on his chest. She slept peacefully, making an occasional deep breathing sound. That was probably as close to snoring as she would ever get.

It felt so right to have her in his arms. He'd never needed anyone in his life, but last night he'd needed her. It wasn't sexual, either. Not that he didn't want her. But last night was about something entirely different—comfort, caring and mental nourishment so he could face another day. Holding on to Alex gave him that strength.

She stirred and sat up, brushing the hair out of her eyes. "Good morning," she whispered.

He felt a catch in his gut at her sleep-filled voice. Her soft brown eyes were languid, sensuous, and he had a feeling she'd look like this after making love.

Raising himself to a sitting position, he flexed his shoulders. "Morning."

She sniffed the air. "I don't smell coffee. After spending the night on the sofa, I expect coffee to be brought to me." Her eyes twinkled.

"I'm not used to getting coffee for a woman."

"Cowboy, that is so hard to believe."

He tucked a stray hair behind her ear. "I'll bring you coffee any day of the week."

Dear Reader,

Saying goodbye to my rodeo cowboys is enough to break a girl's heart. *Once a Cowboy* is the bull rider Brodie's story. He's the last of the three cowboys I first wrote about in *The Christmas Cradle* (HAR, November 2004) and *The Cowboy's Return* (HAR, February 2006).

Brodie is tough and fearless. After all, he rode enormous, angry bucking bulls for a living. I kept asking myself two questions before I started writing his story. The first was what's his Achilles' heel? That chink in his armor of strength? The answer was his family—probably like a lot of us. With his family he never felt as if he fit in, but with his rodeo friends he feels at home.

The next question was what would a man like Brodie do when a pretty P.I., Alex Donovan, comes into his life and tells him that his DNA says he's someone else? At fifteen or twenty I figured he would be angry and resentful and hell-bent on a life of rebellion. But Brodie is forty and more mature. How would he react? And how would he deal with the persistent P.I.? You'll have to keep reading to find the answers.

I have enjoyed creating these cowboys and the women who tame them. So I say goodbye and hope they find a home in your heart.

Warmly,

Linda Warren

It always brightens my day to hear from readers. You can e-mail me at Lw1508@aol.com or write me at P.O. Box 5182, Bryan, TX 77805 or visit my Web site at www.lindawarren.net or superauthors.com. Your letters will be answered.

Once A Cowboy
LINDA WARREN

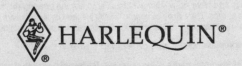

TORONTO • NEW YORK • LONDON
AMSTERDAM • PARIS • SYDNEY • HAMBURG
STOCKHOLM • ATHENS • TOKYO • MILAN • MADRID
PRAGUE • WARSAW • BUDAPEST • AUCKLAND

ISBN-13: 978-0-373-75155-6
ISBN-10:   0-373-75155-9

ONCE A COWBOY

This book is dedicated to my wonderful editor,
Kathleen Scheibling. You've made the
past three years a joy. Thank you.

Books by Linda Warren

HARLEQUIN AMERICAN ROMANCE

HARLEQUIN SUPERROMANCE

ABOUT THE AUTHOR

A Waldenbooks series bestselling writer, Linda Warren is the award-winning author of sixteen books for Harlequin Superromance and Harlequin American Romance. She grew up in the farming and ranching community of Smetana, Texas, the only girl in a family of boys. She loves to write about Texas, and from time to time scenes and characters from her childhood show up in her books. Linda lives in College Station, Texas, not far from her birthplace, with her husband, Billy, and a menagerie of wild animals, from Canada geese to bobcats. Visit her Web site at www.lindawarren.net.

Chapter One

The defunct air-conditioning spit out its last puffs of cool air about an hour ago. Since it was July in Dallas the office was hotter than the hinges of hell. An opened window only stoked the heat in the room. Alex Donovan, private investigator, squirmed in her chair and swallowed back a curse word. She never thought being hot could make her so damn irritable.

"I believe this is my son."

The lady sitting across from her desk pushed a dog-eared newspaper clipping toward Alex.

Sweat trickled down Alex's back and pooled at her waistline. One more minute and she would have been out the door. Now she was caught.

Pushing back her frustration with the heat, the office and life in general, she studied the picture of a cowboy astride a bucking bull. The massive black animal looked too menacing to tangle with—that is, to a city girl like Alex. The colored clipping was dated a month ago and was taken at a rodeo for charity in Fort Worth. The caption read: Brodie Hayes, bull rider and three-time world champion gives another stellar performance.

His record was impressive. As was the man himself.

The lady pulled a folder out of her purse—more photos—and carefully laid them in front of Alex. They were of the same man; on a horse, with two other cowboys and one head shot that gave a close-up of his features. Several were rodeo photos with PRCA stamped on them—Professional Rodeo Cowboys Association.

But Alex's eyes were drawn to the clipping of the cowboy on the bull, which best showcased his broad shoulders and long, muscled body. One hand stuck high in the air as he strove to stay on the required eight seconds. His hat lay in the dirt and dark hair fell across his forehead. The sharp angles of his face were set in deep concentration, yet a glimmer of a smile shaped his lips. She had a feeling this man thrived on winning. Thrived on a challenge.

Handsome, tough and *fearless* were the three words that came to her mind. He was also likely a charmer who had a way with the ladies, but was hell in a fight with a man or a bull. Damn. He was good-looking. Heat centered in her lower abdomen and she began to wonder if the high temperature was getting to her brain.

Having lived in Texas all her life, she'd seen lots of cowboys, but none quite like this. What was it about him? He had the looks, definitely the sex appeal, yet there was something else about him that she couldn't define.

Alex glanced at the lady, waiting for her story,

because she knew there was one. The woman had sad green eyes—that was the first thing she'd noticed. A younger woman who looked to be somewhere in her thirties sat beside her. Probably a daughter or a relative because they had the same facial features, except for black hair untouched by gray, and blue eyes.

"My name is Helen Braxton and this is my daughter, Maggie Newton."

"Nice to meet you, Mrs. Braxton. Maggie. You said you thought this was your son?" Alex fingered the clipping and stared at the daughter. The striking color of her eyes held Alex's attention. Baby-blue. The bluest blue—the same as the cowboy's. Or very close.

Mrs. Braxton handed her another folder. "My son was stolen from the hospital when he was two days old. That was almost forty years ago." She tapped the folder. "The information's all in here."

A feeling of déjà vu came over Alex. She'd dealt with cases like this when she was on the Dallas police force, where desperate parents saw the face of their missing child in every newspaper clipping, their fate in every headline.

One particular case still haunted her. The suffering of the parents had gotten to her and she'd put her heart and soul into finding their missing child. She'd given them hope, which was all they had left. But it hadn't been enough.

Was Helen Braxton one of those parents? Even after forty years, was hope all she had?

Alex licked her dry lips. "Why do you think this is your son?"

Mrs. Braxton dug in her bag and Alex wondered

what else she had in that suitcase of a purse. She laid three photos on the desk while juggling the purse on her lap. "After I saw the photo in the paper, I couldn't get it out of my mind. I checked out Mr. Hayes on the Internet. I bugged Maggie until she helped. That's how I got all the photos." She pointed to the pictures on the desk. "This is my husband and my other two sons. Look at them, then look at the cowboy."

Alex did as instructed and saw they indeed shared a striking resemblance—the same structure of the face, the same black hair. But it was the eyes that affected her the most. They had a bluer than blue quality—as clear and as riveting as the beaches of Padre Island. From the close-up of the cowboy she could see that his eyes were the same. Just like Maggie's.

"We named our first son Travis, after my husband. Maggie is our second child, then we had Wesley and Will. Will drowned when he was nineteen and we lost Wes a year ago. His truck was hit by a drunken driver and…" She pulled a tissue out of the bag and dabbed at her eyes. "Wes helped run the ranch, and now my husband has sunk so far into depression that neither my daughter nor I can reach him." Her watery eyes looked directly at Alex. "Ms. Donovan, please, I need you to find my only remaining son."

The plea in the woman's voice worked to accomplish what her father always warned her about—it touched her heart.

Mrs. Braxton fished out a checkbook. "What do you charge? We don't have much, but we'll pay whatever you ask."

Alex had to be completely honest. "Mrs. Braxton. The odds that this man is your son are very low." She clasped her hands on the desk and felt the waistband of her jeans stick to her skin. Couldn't they feel the heat? Neither seemed bothered by it.

"I've tried to tell her that, but she won't listen to me." These were the first words the daughter had spoken.

"I know I'm a foolish old woman," Mrs. Braxton said. "I have to know, though, why he looks so much like my husband and my other sons. It's been almost forty years and not a day goes by that I don't think about Travis. When he was kidnapped, there was a huge investigation. My husband and I haunted the police station, but our baby had disappeared without a trace."

She twisted the strap of her purse. "The detective said that most babies are found within twenty-four hours because the perpetrator is usually a woman who's desperate for a child and she's eager to show off the baby. Friends and neighbors usually recognize the person wasn't pregnant and contact the authorities. We waited and waited but no such person was ever found. Every lead was a dead end. For years we hounded the detective and he finally told us that we needed to go on with our lives. I laughed at him. How do you go on without your child?"

Helen blinked back a tear. "But life did go on. I had other children and tried to have a normal life for them. Every so often something happens, though, like seeing this photo in the paper, that gives me hope that some day I will see my son."

"Mrs. Braxton..."

"He lives somewhere around Mesquite. That shouldn't be too hard to check out."

The sad eyes now turned desperate and Alex felt herself being pulled in against her will. So much heartache for one family.

"They do a lot of things with DNA these days. A simple test is all I'm asking."

Say no. Just say no. But somehow Alex found she couldn't. She scooted closer to the edge of her chair. Something about Helen's sad eyes was about to make her break one of Buck's cardinal rules. *Do not get emotionally involved.*

She'd been told her head was as hard as a crowbar, but this wasn't about being stubborn or strong-willed. This was about proving she could take the difficult cases and stay emotionally detached. This was her own personal test.

"You do realize we'd be invading this man's privacy, turning his world upside down."

"But you're a detective. Can't you do it discreetly?"

"Yes, but…"

"Just name your price. I'll write you a check."

"Mom, please." Maggie touched her mother's arm.

Mrs. Braxton covered her daughter's hand for a moment, then glanced at Alex. "Ms. Donovan, this is my last chance to save my husband, my family and my sanity." She pointed to the clipping. "That is my son. I just know it. I've been looking for years and I've never had this feeling before. Please."

Buck had warned her about taking these types of cases, but she never paid too much attention to her father—her partner in the agency. He'd say they were too emotional and too time-consuming. Tell her that she shouldn't put herself through that again. To go with the cases that bring in the big bucks and leave the gut-wrenching cases to detectives with more grit in their gizzards.

In his own way, she knew her father was trying to keep her from getting hurt again. While working on the Dallas police force she'd found a missing child murdered. She realized then she didn't have steel-coated nerves. It had been a tough decision to quit the force and join her father in the detective agency. If she wanted to be tough as nails, she had the perfect teacher—Buck Donovan. But she hadn't worked a missing person's case since. It was time to get back into the swing of things.

She stared at the photo of Brodie Hayes. There had to be a way to do this discreetly and put Mrs. Braxton's mind at rest once and for all. And she could make sure that no one got hurt, especially one very good-looking cowboy.

"I'll do some checking, but I'm not promising anything." Alex told her the retainer fee and Mrs. Braxton wrote out a check.

"Oh, thank you, Ms. Donovan." Relief filled Mrs. Braxton's face and Alex wished with all her heart this case would turn out the way the woman wanted. The odds were against her. Still, she'd do her best.

"Please call me Alex." She rose and was grateful for the flurry of air the movement circulated.

"And please call me Helen." Helen slipped the strap of her purse over her arm. "My phone number and everything is in the folder."

"Thank you. I'll be in touch." Helen walked out, but Maggie lingered.

"Ms.—Alex, my parents don't have a lot of money. My father used to raise cutting horses, but after Wes's death he sold most of them. They live off their social security now. I'm powerless to stop my mother in this search. Since we lost Wes, it consumes her whole life. And when she saw the photo, well, our lives haven't been the same."

"I can imagine that losing a child is something a woman never gets over."

Maggie brushed back her dark hair. "Yes. I have two children, a son, Cody, and a daughter, Amber. If someone took them from me, I'm not sure how I would handle it."

"Your mother seems very strong."

"Yes, but please don't indulge this fantasy of hers. Travis is gone and I…we have to accept that. After all these years my mother has to find a way to let him go." Her blue eyes pleaded for Alex to understand.

"I'll do my research and be very honest about my findings."

"Thank you." She turned to leave, then reached into the pocket of her two-piece suit. "I live here in Dallas and my parents live in Weatherford. Here are my numbers." Maggie laid a card on the desk. "If you find anything, please call me first so I can be with my mother when you tell her."

"I will," Alex promised, and Maggie walked out.

She studied the card—an accountant. What a load Maggie carried being the only remaining child. That had to be hard for her, but she also seemed like a strong woman.

Alex gathered everything and put it in her briefcase. Her goal now was to breathe fresh air—cool fresh air.

The offices consisted of four rooms—a reception area, her father's office and hers, then a storage room. With her briefcase in hand, she headed for the front door. It opened before she reached it and her father, Dirk Donovan, walked in.

"What the hell? It's like an oven in here. Why in the hell don't you have on the air-conditioning?"

Buck, as he was called, was an ex-police officer who stood over six feet and had a hefty frame and a sour disposition. To say they never saw eye-to-eye on anything was an understatement. Sometimes Alex questioned her sanity in going into partnership with him, but after her last assignment with the Dallas police department she needed someone who would not treat her with kid gloves. Buck certainly had never done that.

And a part of her was searching for a closer relationship with her father. She felt she barely knew this man who most people seemed to fear, including her at times. Her mother died when Alex was two so she never knew her. She yearned for a family connection, a normal life and a deeper father-daughter relationship.

They'd been partners for two years and Buck criticized, ridiculed and browbeat her at every turn. She gave as good as she got, but what did that say about her—that she was a glutton for punishment? Or maybe, like Mrs. Braxton, she still believed in fantasy, fairy tales and a happy ending.

She placed one hand on her hip. "You're a detective. Can't you figure out why it's so hot in here?"

"Damn. It's out again."

"You got it."

Buck swiped an arm across his forehead. "Did you call that damn repair man?"

She took a long breath. "Yes. Bert said he'd be here in the morning."

"In the morning!" The earsplitting exclamation almost shifted the pictures on the walls. "What the hell's the matter with him?"

"It's July in Texas. He's busy."

"You have to learn to push, girl. You're too damn soft. How many times do I have to tell you that?"

She kept her temper in check. "Feel free to push all you want. I'm going home where it's cool."

"Bert'll have his ass over here by this afternoon." Buck headed for his office, then stopped. "Who were those women I saw leaving?"

"Mrs. Helen Braxton and her daughter. She hired me to find her son."

"What?" One eyebrow jerked upward in surprise.

"Her son was stolen from a hospital almost forty years ago when he was two days old."

"Oh, for crying out loud. Why would you take such a case? Call her and tell her you've changed your mind. We're working on those cases for the district attorney and that's where our attention should be—where the money is. Get your head out of the clouds."

She stiffened her backbone, which was an effort in the heat. "I have no intention of doing any such thing."

"Don't talk back to me, girl. Just do what I tell you. You put yourself through hell when you found that murdered girl. A cop learns never to put his heart into those kinds of cases, but you had to learn the hard way."

She gritted her teeth until her jaw ached. "Yes. I did, but I don't regret my involvement in the Woodly case. The perpetrator is behind bars for the rest of his insane life and the parents have finally moved on. They had another child last year. I get a card every Christmas from them. You're right, though. I do get emotionally involved, but I'm older now and much stronger, especially after working with you."

He nodded, taking the words as a compliment. "I told you I'd put some grit in your gizzard."

Alex grimaced. "That sounds very painful. I'd rather have chocolate in my gizzard; it's a whole lot sweeter."

"Heaven forbid." Buck rolled his eyes. "Women!"

"And just so you understand me—I'll work on any case I want. If I get emotionally involved, well, that's my choice."

Her response was met with a scowl, but no scathing remarks were forthcoming.

"Mrs. Braxton thinks she's already found her son. I just have to prove that this man is or isn't the right man. Very easy case."

"Just make sure it doesn't interfere with our work."

"I'll do it in my spare time. It's not like I have a social life or a family."

"If you moved out on your own, maybe you would."

"And who would keep you and Naddy from killing each other?"

"Your grandmother can hold her own, she doesn't need you to protect her."

Nadene and Buck did not have a typical mother-son relationship. Buck was the result of a teenage pregnancy and Naddy had been married so many times that it was hard to keep track.

Her grandmother drank, smoked and loved to have a good time. Though Buck was a lot like her, he did not appreciate those qualities in his mother. As a bail bondsman, Naddy had led a colorful life. At seventy-eight, she was now retired. Her days were spent surfing the Internet for criminals. She did a lot of research on missing children and had even helped to find a couple.

When Alex was younger she used to wish her grandmother was more conventional, yet she had always been comforted by the thought that whatever she had to go through in this world, Naddy would be behind her all the way.

"Thought the old battle-ax would have moved out by now." Buck's voice brought her back to the conversation. "Hell, she's gone ten years without getting married. That has to be a record."

"She's getting older. I think Naddy is with us to stay."

"Ain't that a helluva thing. She was never there for me as a kid and now I'm supposed to take care of her."

Alex watched the man who was her father. With his crew cut hairstyle, shaggy gray eyebrows, slant for a mouth and sagging features, Buck Donovan was as hard as they come. Naddy had a part in making him that way but Alex wondered what kind of feelings he had for her, his own daughter. Buck probably couldn't define them himself. And asking him would be a mortal sin, she was sure.

She caught his eyes. "She was there for me when my mother died. Doesn't that count for something?"

"Maybe. Might be the only reason she's still in my house."

That comment was like a crumb to a starving person and she savored it as such. Those crumbs were few and far between.

"I'll see you at home."

Was she pathetic or what? Thirty-four years old and still living at home with her father and her grandmother. She needed a life. Bad.

SHE NEGOTIATED the Dallas traffic the same way she'd handled her father—with a large dose of patience and gritted teeth. She turned off US-75 and headed for the Lake Highlands suburb where they lived, her body greedily soaking up the coolness of the car's air-conditioning.

She had a love-hate relationship with the Texas summers. She loved them when she was relaxing on the beach in Galveston or Padre Island, but she hated them in the trenches of Dallas. There weren't many opportunities to get away for a weekend—Buck believed in her keeping her nose to the grindstone— but if she could find one, she'd take it. All her girl-friends were married, though, and had families. Her relationship with her cop boyfriend, Clay, had ended about a year ago.

Single, unattached and feeling my age. Maybe she should have that made into a bumper sticker. Or, better, *single and available.* That would certainly draw attention.

She turned into the driveway with a smile. Getting

out, she glanced at the rows of brick houses built in the sixties. Buck and her mother Joan had bought their house right after they'd married. They had a large corner lot and Buck had a shop in back where he kept his boat and fishing paraphernalia.

White Rock Lake wasn't far away and when she was younger she'd spent a lot of time hanging out at the lake with her friends. This had been Alex's home all her life, but she knew it was time for her to move on—perhaps to find that elusive happiness she'd always been searching for.

Placing her purse and briefcase on the hood of her Jeep Wrangler, she turned on the sprinkler for the wilted Saint Augustine grass, making sure the water reached the blooming crepe myrtles. Alex took care of the yard. Any calls for help from Buck or Naddy she found to be a waste of her time. The sun beat down on her bare head and after the heat of the morning she did something she wouldn't normally do. She ran through the sprinkler, laughing not caring if the neighbors were watching.

By the time she entered the house, her skin was almost dry. Her clothes were damp from sweat so the extra water didn't make a difference. The air-conditioning felt wonderful on her wet skin. Pure bliss.

Laying her things on the kitchen table, she saw Naddy sitting at her computer through the open door of her bedroom. Buck's bedroom was on the right side of the house and Naddy's on the left, a house clearly divided. Alex occupied the bedroom upstairs and had her private space.

"Hey, Naddy, I'm home," she called, grabbing a Popsicle out of the freezer.

"Come here, honeychild. I want to show you something."

Alex walked to Naddy's bedroom, licking on the icy treat. It was her favorite snack in the summertime, cool, refreshing and... She stopped in Naddy's doorway. Her bedroom was a disaster. She really shouldn't be surprised because Naddy tended not to pick up anything.

Buck, on the other hand, was neat and organized. A gene he obviously got from his "low-life loser father" as Naddy often said.

Alex stepped over a pile of dirty clothes. Trying to change her grandmother would be like trying to change the course of the wind or the Texas heat.

"What?" Alex asked, trying to ignore the dirty clothes hanging off of chairs and lying all over the floor. The tumbled sheets partially hid an empty Doritos bag. A couple of empty beer cans stood on the nightstand beside a jar of nuts.

"Look." Naddy pointed to the screen, squinting at it through the glasses perched on her nose. A tall, big-boned woman, Naddy once had sandy red hair. Now it was completely white, short and stuck out in all directions, mainly because Naddy always forgot to comb it. Her skin was leathery and wrinkled, the skin of a smoker. An unlit cigarette dangled from her lip.

"Why is there a cigarette in your mouth?" Buck had strict rules about smoking in the house. Joan had made them when Alex was born and Buck kept to them, even though he smoked. He always smoked outdoors and Alex had a feeling he adhered to the rule to annoy Naddy.

"Keep your britches on, honeychild. I was going outside to light up when I found this. Tell me what you think. The baby on the left disappeared fourteen years ago in Houston. The girl on the right was found dead in an alley in Vegas last week. Look at the faces. I think it's the same girl." Her voice was excited.

Alex studied the faces. "Very similar."

"I want to contact the authorities in Vegas, but I need a drag first." Naddy stood and brushed crumbs off of her flowered housedress. "What are you doing home this time of the day and why are you all wet?"

Alex took a bite of the Popsicle. "The air's out again."

Naddy smiled. "Biting that Popsicle reminds me of when you were six years old. I'd tell you not to eat them so fast that they'd give you a headache, but you never listened."

"I think I'm always going to be six years old," she replied in a melancholy voice. *Living at home and yearning for love.*

"Bite your tongue." Naddy rummaged through a stack of papers on her desk. "Ethel's grandson is in town and I told her you'd go out with him."

Alex shook her head. "No. You are not setting me up for another date. Never again will I do that. I can get my own dates, thank you."

Naddy looked indignant. "What was wrong with the last date I got you?"

"He brought his mother with him."

Naddy grimaced. "Oh, yeah. That was out of the ordinary."

"And stupid, insane, weird, creepy and…"

"Okay, okay. I'll stay out of your affairs. I don't have good taste in men anyway."

"Amen."

They eyed each other and laughed, then Alex hugged her grandmother. That was one of the things she loved about Naddy. She brought laughter to Alex's life.

Naddy drew back. "Your skin is hot."

"I've been sitting in a oven, which is what the office is at the moment."

"That cheapskate son of mine needs to put in a new unit."

Alex shrugged. "You know Buck."

Naddy pushed her glasses up the bridge of her nose. "Hmmph."

"Good luck identifying the girl." Alex glanced around the room. "Tonight we're doing laundry and maybe we'll fumigate this room."

"Yeah. Whatever. But first I have to keep digging on the Vegas case until I annoy the hell out of somebody, then they'll pay attention to me." Naddy hurried out of the room to smoke her cigarette.

Naddy had bulldog instincts, just like her son, and most of the time she got results. Alex had a feeling she got her caring gene from Naddy. Her grandmother was always trying to help people.

Alex retrieved her briefcase and purse and headed upstairs to take a shower and to work. By late afternoon

she had a lot of information on Brodie Hayes. He'd
earned lots of accolades. His bull-riding career started
in high school. Even while attending Texas A&M Uni-
versity he kept riding and winning. At nineteen he went
professional. All sorts of endorsements came his way including Wrangler, Budweiser and Ford trucks. Brodie
Hayes seemed to have it all. He retired years ago and
now owned a ranch, like Helen had said. He was single
and had never been married.

Staring at his picture, she found that fact more than
interesting. Why was a handsome hunk like that still unattached? One answer came to mind, but she pushed it
away. He was too masculine and… That meant absolutely nothing. She kept searching.

His father was a general in the U.S. Army and his
mother was an army wife who followed her husband all
over the world. Nothing about his life looked out of the
ordinary, but one thing caught Alex's attention. Travis
Braxton was born five days after Brodie Hayes in the
same hospital in Dallas. How weird was that? Could that
just be a coincidence?

She mulled this over for about thirty minutes, then
she knew what she had to do. She had Brodie Hayes's
address and somehow, someway she would get a DNA
sample from him.

Chapter Two

Alex had told Mrs. Braxton that she could handle the investigation discreetly and that's what she planned to do. First, she would meet Brodie Hayes and take it from there.

Finding his ranch wasn't a problem—she'd gotten the exact directions from the Internet. She took I-635 then US-80 and traveled down a blacktop road until she reached the entrance to the Cowboy Up Ranch. Driving over a cattle guard, she noticed red-and-white-faced cattle lying beneath oak trees. Others were grazing in the heat or drinking from a water trough.

A ranch-style frame house loomed in front of her, a pipe fence separating it from the pasture. There were corrals and barns to the right. Everything was quiet, no activity anywhere. She parked on the side of the house and got out. Two gray-and-white dogs loped toward her.

Her breath wedged in her throat as they sniffed at her feet. "Hi there," she said. The dogs barked and she forced herself not to show fear or jump back. "Hello to you, too," she responded as brightly as she could. When the dogs trotted back to the barn, she let out a tight breath. Evidently they didn't consider her a threat. Thank God.

She walked up the stone walk to the door. There was no doorbell, so she knocked.

The wooden veranda-type porch stretched along the front of the white house. Horseshoes welded together made sturdy columns. Two wrought-iron chairs with denim seats graced both sides of the door. An inviting swing hung from the rafters. Although shrubbery grew against the house, the neatly mowed yard showed no signs of flowers or flowerbeds. All telltale signs this was the home of a bachelor.

No one came to the door. The thought of breaking in crossed her mind. She could be in and out in less than two minutes with something with his DNA on it, but she wasn't quite ready to go to those lengths. When she was about to give up she saw a white pickup barreling her way.

She just got lucky.

BRODIE HAYES had had one of those days and he was relieved to get back to his place, his own home. Spending time with his mother left him feeling as if he'd been kicked in the stomach by a two-thousand-pound bull. He was raw, sore and a little dazed.

His parents had never understood him and the years hadn't made a difference. He was always acutely aware that he was a big disappointment to both of them.

At five, Brodie was riding his mother's broom as a horse. His father took it away from him and made him use it as a gun. As a kid he didn't understand that—he didn't want a gun. He wanted to ride a horse. When he was six, he asked Santa for cowboy boots. He didn't get them and he stopped believing in Santa Claus.

The years his father was stationed at Fort Hood, Texas, were the happiest time of Brodie's life. He'd made a friend, Colter Kincaid, whose family lived on a ranch and Brodie loved to visit. He learned to ride a horse and he went to rodeos with them. Following that first rodeo, he was hooked. The massive bulls held his attention. He and Colter started riding in the junior rodeos. To enter, Brodie forged his father's signature because he knew his parents wouldn't approve.

That first ride he was bucked into the dirt so hard that the wind left his body. But that only spurred his interest, making him determined to complete the eight-second ride. He would secretly enter the local rodeos, never telling his parents how he was spending his spare time. When Brodie started to win, he didn't count on the news being in the papers.

His father was furious and grounded him. Tom Hayes believed in strict discipline and lying was definitely against the family rules. Brodie caved into the pressure and agreed to apply to Texas A&M. He majored in agriculture economics, much to his father's disapproval.

In college he rodeoed on the weekends and he told his parents. They didn't like it, but as long as he was in college they didn't complain. And Brodie had turned eighteen so his decisions were his own. As he kept winning he knew what he wanted to do with his life. Tom's wishes were for Brodie to go into the army, but Brodie knew that life wasn't for him.

His parents pressured Brodie every way they could,

but at nineteen he quit college and followed the rodeo circuit. He made friends who became his family. Colter Kincaid had also decided the rodeo was the life for him. To Brodie, Colter and another cowboy named Tripp Daniels were like his brothers. They always would be.

His parents finally accepted his rodeo ways, as they called his life, but they had very little contact during those years. His father relented enough to fly to Vegas when Brodie won the national finals. They had a congratulatory beer together before his father left for Washington. He died two months later.

Claudia, his mother, moved to Dallas to be near her sister, Cleo. They were an unlikely pair. His mother was a social butterfly, enjoying teas, luncheons and charity functions. Cleo, who had married beneath her, as his mother had so often said, had been a cook in a large restaurant until she retired. Claudia had never approved of Cleo's lifestyle—Cleo had been married three times and she loved to dance and go out and have fun. That was what had caused the problem today.

Brodie had lunch with them once a week. Cleo was a great cook and he always enjoyed the meal, but his mother was in one of her moods. Cleo had a new boyfriend and they went square-dancing several nights a week. Claudia was upset because that left her alone at night. She wanted Brodie to tell Cleo how bad this man was for her. He didn't even know the man and he had no intention of doing any such thing.

When he refused, his mother had become suddenly short of breath. Claudia had had rheumatic fever as a child that left her with a heart murmur. After Brodie's birth, she began to have more and more problems with her heart. Two years ago, she'd had a mild heart attack, and today he'd feared the same thing was happening.

He'd spent the rest of the afternoon in the emergency room and the doctor said Claudia didn't have a heart attack, just an anxiety attack. In the end, his mother had gotten what she'd wanted—Cleo would stay home to take care of Claudia.

His mother had always been clingy and needy and it seemed to have gotten worse with age. Soon he'd have to talk to her about her fear of being alone. He wasn't looking forward to it. The bruises were still too raw from today's confrontation.

He'd rather face a bull from the bowels of hell than have a conversation with his mother. He knew he had a chance of surviving with the bull. Claudia had a way of ripping him to shreds with just a few well-chosen words.

He frowned as he saw a Jeep parked in his driveway. He didn't recognize it, then he saw a woman walking toward the vehicle. A blonde in white shorts that showed off long, slim legs and a tank top that bared tanned arms. Her hair was clipped behind her head and those feminine curves were in all the right places. Touchable places.

His day just got better.

THE WHITE FOUR-DOOR TRUCK rattled loudly so Alex knew it was a diesel. The large grill guard and all-terrain tires indicated the truck was for heavy-duty jobs. A man and his truck. In Texas, it defined who he was. This truck said Brodie Hayes was one tough hombre. A woman raised in Texas knew to never mess with a man's truck or his life. Alex was about to break one of those rules.

The dogs trotted from the barn and scurried to her, sniffing at her feet again. She hardly noticed them as she watched one booted foot slide to the ground. She held her breath as she waited for the rest of the cowboy to emerge from the truck. Tight-fitting Wranglers molded his long legs, a gold belt buckle glistened on a tooled leather belt, a starched white shirt framed his broad shoulders and a Stetson rested perfectly on his dark head. She found herself staring into the bluest eyes she'd ever seen. The bluest eyes in Texas, she thought, her pulse hammering wildly in her ears.

He removed his hat. "Howdy, ma'am. May I help you?"

Ohmygod. He had a dimple in the carved structure of his left cheek—an incredibly sexy dimple. His black hair curled into his collar in an unruly, wanton way. The heat of the sun was hot, but this sensual type of heat was much hotter. It burned through her body all the way to her toes and she curled them into her sandals.

Looking at his picture was one thing, but seeing him in the flesh was quite another. A neon sign seemed to blink in her mind. *Cowboy. Dangerous. Stay away.*

For the first time she was physically attracted to a man just by looking at him. She always thought that type of reaction was crazy when her girlfriends had giggled about it. Of course she'd found men handsome, but she'd never sleep with them just because of that. Brodie Hayes was different. With the crook of his finger…she drew in a deep breath. Weak and pliable she wasn't.

"Ma'am?"

His voice was deep with a true Texas drawl that tightened her toes even more and sent her pulse into orbit. But somehow she managed to find her vocal cords.

"I was looking for the Circle C Ranch." As a private investigator, she was used to thinking fast.

He shook his head. "Never heard of it."

"I must have gotten the directions wrong." She hated to play stupid, but sometimes it worked. "I'll call my friend to see where I turned wrong."

He just dipped his head in acknowledgement.

She'd hoped for some sort of conversation or introduction, but none came so she walked toward her car. She had no intention of leaving though. Getting in, she waited until he disappeared inside. Large oak trees shaded the house and the dogs trotted to one and lay down. A light breeze stirred the stifling heat.

A plan formed in her mind. If she could get something with his DNA on it, then Brodie wouldn't have to know about Helen Braxton. It would save him some heartache. Counting to ten, she got out, marched to the front door and knocked.

He opened it immediately and her heart did a nervous flip-flop. If they could package masculinity, Brodie Hayes's picture would be on the bottle. She was getting tired of that female reaction. He probably encountered it every day. He was just a man. Get over it, she told herself. She had a job to do.

"I'm sorry to bother you again, but my cell's not working. May I please use your phone?"

"Sure." He opened the door wider and she stepped into his home. She followed him through a foyer into a large den with a stone fireplace, hardwood floors and overstuffed leather furniture. A large plasma TV almost covered one wall and plaques, trophies, belt buckles and numerous items from his rodeo days were displayed in a large glass case that covered another wall.

She was taking in her surroundings, but trying to be discreet when he handed her a cordless phone.

"Thank you. I don't know what's wrong with my cell. I can't get a signal."

"That happens sometimes."

She was getting the impression he was a man of few words. Engaging in a friendly chat wasn't going to happen. Why wasn't he curious or intrigued by a strange woman on his doorstep?

She had no choice but to place a call. She poked out her home number, hoping Naddy would be outside smoking another cigarette. Her luck didn't hold. Naddy answered on the second ring.

"Nad, this is Alex. I'm afraid I'm lost. Could you please give me the directions again?"

"Who is this?" She heard the confusion in Naddy's voice.

"Yes, I know. I'm always getting lost. But I'm a city girl and these country roads are so confusing."

"I'm hanging up because you're not making any sense. I get confused enough on my own."

"You know me, and please don't use a dumb blonde joke."

"Oh. You're stalling for time or staking out a place somewhere." Bless her, Naddy finally got it.

"Yes. I'll call you as soon as I get there."

"Whatever, child. I got work to do."

Naddy hung up and Alex did the same, handing the phone to Brodie, who had clicked on the six o'clock news. She hadn't even made a blip on his male radar. Her fragile ego took a nosedive and she brought her thoughts back to the job she was here to do. Get DNA evidence.

"Thank you," she said, her eyes trailing toward the rodeo memorabilia. "Are those yours?"

He glanced at her. "Yes."

She walked closer, staring at several silver and gold buckles. "So you're a rodeo rider?"

"Used to be. Just a cowboy now. "

She held out her hand. "I'm Alex Donovan."

Brodie took her hand, it was soft yet strong. Just like the lady, he thought. The moment he looked into her brown eyes he knew she wasn't a casual type gal. "Nice girl" was written all over her pretty face—this was the type of woman he normally steered clear of. Women who wanted commitment, forever and a part of his soul in the bargain.

He chose women who didn't get their hearts broken when he walked away, because that's who he was—a walk-away type guy. His friends, Colter and Tripp, had found true love but he knew that wasn't in the cards for him. Nesting wasn't in his nature. Risking his life and staying on the move was. His father had said those were the qualities of a soldier, but he was a cowboy to the core.

Although it was true that these days he'd settled in one place. Risking his life was a day on the freeway pulling a horse trailer. Since his retirement from the rodeo, his life had changed, he had to admit that. But the woman hadn't been made who could make him think about marriage.

Pity, he thought for a nostalgic moment, the blonde was very attractive. And something about the touch of her smooth skin against his sent his thoughts in an entirely different direction.

He released her hand. "I'm Brodie Hayes."

"Nice to meet you." Her smile lit up her face. Damn. She wasn't just attractive. She was beautiful.

"I apologize for interrupting your evening." She glanced at the TV.

The rise and fall of her breasts against the tank top caught his eye. He pulled himself up sharp. What was wrong with him? This woman wasn't his type.

"No problem, ma'am." He turned his attention back to the TV.

"May I please use your bathroom?"

"Down the hall to the right." He breathed a sigh of relief as she disappeared.

ALEX HURRIED to the bathroom, locked the door and went to work. She was looking for some of his hair. Bingo. A comb lay on the vanity with black strands in it. Not many, but it might be enough.

Pulling a plastic bag out of her pocket, she slipped the comb into it, then tucked it into her shorts. She flushed the commode and quickly made her way to the den.

Brodie had his eyes on the TV and didn't even look up.

"Thank you," she said.

"Sure," he replied, sparing her a brief glance.

She had no choice but to leave. He could have been friendlier. She fumed about that all the way to her car. He was probably used to having his pick of women and today he just wasn't interested. Or he wasn't interested in her. Why did that hurt?

She'd just invaded his privacy and had stolen something from his house, so if she never saw him again that would probably be for the best—for both of them.

All the way into the city, she knew she had the evidence to prove if Brodie Hayes was Helen Braxton's son. She'd told Helen the odds were slim and she still believed that.

But those blue eyes were hard to ignore.

The same eyes she'd seen in the photos of the Braxton men. And in Maggie.

FROM HIS KITCHEN WINDOW, Brodie watched her drive away. He wasn't sure what that was about, but he had a feeling the lady wasn't lost. What was she after? Didn't matter. He'd never see her again.

A smile tugged at his mouth. Tripp would laugh at him. Brodie was known as a charmer, a ladies' man around the rodeo circuit. He never met a woman he didn't like. Or who didn't like him. So what had held him back with...what did she say her name was? Alex Donovan. That was it. What held him back from getting to know Alex better?

He walked into the den and sank into his chair. Maybe he was getting older. Maybe a nice girl wasn't on his to-do list. Or maybe his instincts told him Alex deserved better than a walk-away cowboy.

ALEX CAME THROUGH the back door and did a double take. Naddy, with her hair in rollers, was in the utility room, stuffing clothes into the washing machine.

"Get your investigating done?" Naddy asked, pouring soap onto the clothes.

"Yes. Thanks for catching on."

"Might take me a minute, but I always catch on." Naddy closed the lid.

"Naddy, what are you doing?"

Naddy lifted a sharp eyebrow.

"Okay. Dumb question. I'll try again. Why are you washing clothes? I usually have to threaten you to get you to do that."

"I'm going to Vegas and I need clean clothes." Naddy turned the dial and water spewed into the machine. Alex couldn't hear over the loud noise so she pulled her grandmother into the kitchen.

"Why are you going to Vegas?"

"Can't get those idiots in control of the case to listen to me. I'm going in person. Ethel and me are driving."

"What!" Alex followed her into her bedroom. "You are *not* driving to Vegas. Absolutely not."

"I drive just as good as when I was twenty, only better. I don't drive as fast."

Alex took a calming breath. "You're not driving to Vegas in your old Buick."

Naddy placed her hands on her hips. "Are you saying that I'm old?"

"You're seventy-eight. What do you think?"

"I think I can do what I want."

"Naddy…"

"Ethel's seventy-six and she doesn't drive too bad, except she has trouble staying awake."

"Okay. Okay." Alex threw up her hands, knowing her grandmother was working her. "I'll pay for your plane ticket."

"What about Ethel? I don't want to go alone."

Alex gritted her teeth. "Okay. I'll pay for Ethel, too."

"You're such a sucker." Naddy laughed.

"I knew you were playing me from the start. You wouldn't do laundry unless you were after something. And you'd better not crow too much or I'll rescind the offer." She paused. "Does Buck know you're going?"

"No. You can tell him after I'm gone."

Alex shook her head. "Oh, no. You tell him before you leave."

"Honeychild." Naddy put an arm around her shoulder and Alex caught a whiff of Ben-Gay. "Why do you always want that family connection to be there? It isn't. I was a bad mother, a terrible mother. I admit that. Bucky has a right to hate me. I was young, stupid and had no idea how to raise a kid. He grew up the hard way, by himself with a string of step-daddies."

Alex had heard this a million times and Naddy wasn't getting around her by using that bad-mother routine. "All the same, you'll tell him."

"Did I say you were a sucker? Crafty is more like it."

"I'll be upstairs," she said, walking away.

"Want to help with my laundry?"

"No, thanks," Alex called, running up the stairs.

She laid the plastic bag with the comb on her dresser. In the morning she'd call a lab they used to run the test.

She'd also call Helen so she could give a sample to see if Brodie was her son. One little test, but it could change a lot of lives.

That night she went to sleep seeing the bluest eyes in Texas.

THE NEXT MORNING she awoke to loud voices, which was reminiscent of her childhood. Evidently Naddy had told Buck she was going to Vegas. She didn't bother going down. They'd yell and scream until one of them was out of breath.

She changed into jeans and a knit top. She brushed her hair and clipped it behind her head. After applying the barest of makeup, she headed downstairs.

"Don't think I'm paying for this crazy trip!"

"I never asked you for a dime."

"Yeah, right."

Alex walked between Buck and Naddy. "Good morning, all. Think I'll get my coffee on the way to work." With her hand on the doorknob, she looked at her father. "Is the air fixed?"

"I had to work on the damn thing myself and I got it going for now. Bert'll fix it this morning."

"Really? The old push method didn't work?"

Buck glared at her. "Don't start with me. I've already had it with Naddy. Going to Vegas. That's insane." He pointed a finger at his mother. "Don't come back to this house with a man in tow. That's all I got to say."

"Bucky, you take all the fun out of life."

"Don't call me Bucky."

"I had those teeth fixed, didn't I?"

Buck slammed out the door and Alex stared at her grandmother. "This certainly isn't the Cleaver household."

Naddy chuckled. Alex used to sit for hours watching reruns of *Leave It To Beaver,* wishing she had a mother like June and a father like Ward. How unrealistic was that? Not to mention outdated.

"More like a soap opera," Naddy muttered.

Alex only grinned. "When are you leaving?"

"Ethel's daughter is dropping her off and we're taking a cab to the airport."

"Be careful." Alex hugged her.

"If I was careful, I wouldn't have any fun."

Alex smiled on her way out the door.

Buck wasn't in the office so she didn't know where he was, but at least the air was working. She called the lab to set up the DNA test. She dropped the comb off and called Helen, who was eager to help by giving her DNA. Now they waited.

As Alex worked on other cases, she kept thinking about Brodie. Maybe someday she'd have the opportunity to apologize for stealing his comb.

BRODIE WOKE UP to quiet, like always. That's the way he wanted it. His friends called him a people person because he acted outgoing on the rodeo circuit, but he was really a loner. He enjoyed the peace and the quiet. Maybe that had something to do with age, too.

When he was younger, partying was in his blood. The more people around him, the better he liked it. Today life was more sedate and that suited him. He was comfortable with his life choices, but he'd probably always regret the rift with his parents. At least they'd tried to work through it as a family. That was important to him.

He showered and slipped into jeans. After shaving, he reached for his comb, but it wasn't there. He looked in the drawer, then the cabinet. The comb had disappeared. He'd had it yesterday when he'd combed his hair to go see his mother. That was the last time he'd seen it.

No one had been here, not even the cleaning lady. So what could have happened to it? *Wait a minute.* The lady in the Jeep had used his bathroom. Could she have taken his comb? What the hell would she want it for? It didn't make any sense, but he was becoming increasingly intrigued. Why would Alex Donovan steal his comb?

Next time he would be more careful who he let use his bathroom. It was a comb, less than five bucks so what did it matter? Sometimes girls who followed the rodeo circuit would steal an item that belonged to a cowboy they had a crush on just to have something to connect them. But Alex didn't seem like a groupie and she hadn't come on to him. She was friendly, that's all.

So what was going on?

Finding another comb, he finished dressing and headed for the barn. He saddled his horse, Jax, a thoroughbred quarter horse he'd gotten from Colter, who raised them. With the dogs trotting behind him, he checked the herd and all the water troughs to make sure the cattle had water in the searing heat.

Riding gave him peace and he enjoyed the movement, the rhythm, even the sun on his face and the calluses on his hands. He knew who he was—a cowboy in control. As his boots touched soil again the comb business nagged at him.

Suddenly he wanted to find the lady in the Jeep—Alex.

Chapter Three

Brodie arrived at his mother's around ten. Propped up in bed, his petite, fragile mother looked pale yet she seemed much better than yesterday. Cleo fussed about, fluffing pillows and straightening the bed linens.

"Brodie, my son," Claudia said. "I'm sorry I scared you yesterday."

He sat in a Queen Anne chair, his hat in his hand, feeling out of place. "How are you today?"

"Much better."

"She should," Cleo said. "I've been waiting on her hand and foot. You know you're not helpless, Claudie."

Cleo was the antithesis of his mother—she was strong, resilient and resourceful. But Claudia, her older sister, was her Achilles' heel.

"Cleo, please. I don't want to argue today."

"Me, neither. And I don't plan on staying in every night, Claudie, so get used to it." Cleo winked at Brodie. "How about a cup of coffee, cowboy?"

"I'll settle for iced tea."

"You got it."

After Cleo left, Brodie searched for the right words and knew there weren't any. He carefully placed his hat on his knee. "Mother, you can't expect Cleo to stay home all the time. She's sixty-four and enjoys her friends."

"Men friends, you mean."

"Whatever."

"She's been married three times and has absolutely nothing to show for it. You'd think she'd appreciate a roof over her head."

He grabbed his hat and stood in a quick movement because he was about to lose every ounce of patience he'd been blessed with. "Cleo is not your personal slave and she has a right to her own life, whatever that might be."

"You always take her side." Claudia sank farther into the pillows with a hurt expression.

"It's not about sides, Mother." He raked a hand through his hair. "Tell you what. I'll check in to getting someone to stay here when Cleo is out. That way it will be easier for both of you."

"You know you remind me of your father when you do that?"

"What?" He was disconcerted for a moment.

"Your father. Tom always ran a hand through his hair when he was agitated. His hair was dark and thick like yours."

She talked as if he didn't remember his father, but he remembered him very well. When his father crammed a hand through his hair, Brodie quickly disappeared. That meant a stern lecture was about to ensue.

He shook the thought from his mind. "Mother, did you hear what I said?"

"I don't want a stranger in the house. Why can't you stay with me?"

That took the air right out of his chest. He and his mother weren't close. They'd been estranged for a lot of years. When he'd left college, his father had told him to never come back home, that neither he nor Brodie's mother supported his decision to ride professionally. And Brodie was no son of theirs if he chose that life. His mother was always the buffer between Tom and Brodie, but this time she stood stoutly behind her husband's decision.

He knew they thought he would change his mind and they had to be united and strong in their stance. Somewhere inside him he found the courage to walk out the door, realizing he was leaving his childhood behind but hoping to find the man he was supposed to be.

The first two years he had no contact with them at all, then he called home one Christmas. That started periodic phone calls, which usually ended with his mother begging him to stop the silly foolishness of the rodeo. His father's words were always terse. When his father had attended the national finals, they'd finally made their peace. He accepted that Brodie was different than him.

After his father had died and Claudia had moved to Dallas, he and his mother started building a new relationship. Talking to his mother for any length of time had always been a chore for him. The conversation always came around to his choices in life and how bad they were.

Hours with her could make him old before his time.

But she was his mother and he loved her. A few hours weren't going to kill him. Guilt was a powerful thing. It turned cowboys into sissies.

"It's not like you have a wife or anything," Claudia said at his hesitation.

"I have a ranch to run. It's very time-consuming."

"I never understood your interest in cows and horses. I thought you would outgrow it."

He clamped his jaw tight. "No, Mother. That's not going to happen."

"I see that now."

An awkward pause followed.

Claudia tied the bow on her bed jacket. "I am proud of your success, though. Your father was, too."

"Really?" He didn't quite believe that.

"Of course we were. It was just hard for us to accept your lifestyle."

"You make it sound like I was into some sort of deviant behavior." He clenched a fist to keep his cool.

She looked directly at him. "Why do you get so angry when we talk?"

"Maybe because you criticize."

"Do I?" Her green eyes feigned innocence. "I don't mean to."

Brodie had had enough conversation. "It's after ten. Aren't you getting up today?"

"In a little while. Those spells take so much out of me and some days it's just taxing to get out of bed."

"Getting upset doesn't help."

"I know. I'm just a lonely old woman."

The guilt bored into his chest like the horn of a bull.

He bit the bullet and said, "I'll stay with you when Cleo goes out."

Claudia smiled. "Thank you, darling."

He drew a deep breath. "But, Mother, we have to talk about your fear of being alone."

She shifted uneasily in the bed. "You know I've never liked to stay by myself and ever since your father died it's gotten worse. I know it's irrational, but I can't help it."

"Maybe you need to get out more." Recently she hadn't been involved with her social functions.

"Maybe."

"Call your friend Ruth and get back into the bridge group. You always enjoyed playing. And what about the Heart Association fund-raiser and luncheon? That's your pet project and they need your help."

"I'm tired, darling. I think I'll just rest."

For the first time he realized his mother might be going through depression and he planned to mention that to the doctor. He didn't like seeing her this despondent.

BRODIE DECIDED to let Alex keep his comb—for now. He had more pressing matters to deal with. Later, though, he would find out why she saw a need to steal something from his home.

He spent two nights at his mother's watching chick-flick movies. His mother talked about his childhood, his father and her life as an army wife. She talked and he listened. As a single male, he realized this was probably the lowest point in his life—spending evenings with his mother. What had happened to the charmer who had a different woman every night? He'd just hit rock bottom. He had to get his mother back into the swing of living.

THE HOUSE WAS VERY QUIET without Naddy. She'd called and said they'd arrived safely so Alex didn't worry. But with Naddy there was always cause to worry. She tended to do the unexpected.

Alex and Buck finished the cases for the DA and Buck was pleased because in both cases the attorneys were able to secure a guilty verdict.

The DA had its own investigators, but when they needed someone to go the extra mile they knew who to call. Buck was known for getting information out of the person without them knowing it. Everything Alex had learned about investigating, she'd learned from her father.

That morning Buck said, "I'm off to the coast for a few days of fishing."

"Oh?" She looked up from reading the paper.

"Yeah. Bert's putting a new heating-and-cooling unit in so it's no use hanging around here."

"What? You never mentioned that."

"Thought I did."

"No. I would have remembered it."

"Well, you might think about taking some time off, too. We have the Cryder and Wilcox cases next week and we might as well start fresh." He poured another cup of coffee. "I'm going to hook up my boat."

Time off. That sounded wonderful to Alex. She had a friend, Patsy, in Florida she could visit and lie on the beach with drinking piña coladas. As she jumped up to call Patsy, the phone rang.

"Alex, it's Lou at the lab."

This was it. He had the results of the Braxton DNA test. She braced herself.

"I'm sorry. We can't get a clear DNA from Mr. Hayes's hair. We'll need blood or saliva to complete the test."

"Thanks, Lou. I'll get back to you."

She hung up cursing. Damn. This could have been so easy. How was she going to get his blood or saliva? By asking, like she should have done in the first place.

Being discreet had its advantages, but the ethics of this whole situation bothered her. She'd wanted to make things easy for Helen and Brodie—that's the only reason she'd stolen the comb. Ever since she'd done that, though, it had been niggling at her.

She'd have to do this by the book, as Buck had taught her. She'd have to tell Brodie Hayes the truth. He deserved that and it would keep her principles about her job intact. She grabbed her purse, heading for Brodie's ranch once again.

Parking at the house, she spotted him at the corrals on a horse, herding cattle into a pen. Plumes of dust spiraled around him. His truck and trailer were backed up to a loading chute.

Without a second thought she walked to the pipe corral. He dismounted and closed the gate, his gaze swinging to her. His loose-limbed strides brought him closer and she thought again how incredibly sexy he was. Today there were no starched clothes. His chambray shirt and jeans were worn, his boots dusty and his Stetson stained with sweat.

The hat pulled low hid his eyes, but from the firm set of his jaw she knew he wasn't happy to see her.

"You're back," he said, his voice unfriendly.

"May I speak with you please?"

"Lady, I'm rather busy at the moment." Those blue eyes blazed. "And people who steal are not people I want to talk to."

"If you'll give me a few minutes, I can explain."

He seemed to think about it. "You've got five minutes." He meandered around cows to a gate, his dogs behind him. Within seconds, he was standing next to her and his nearness seemed to cut off her breathing.

The heat was suffocating her even more. "Could we sit somewhere?" She blinked against the sun.

He turned toward the barn and she saw a bench beneath an oak tree. She sat down, glad of the shade. He remained standing, staring at her with narrowed eyes. The bluest blue was frosty and she felt a moment of trepidation.

The dogs sniffed at her feet and she patted them. "What's their names?"

"Buck and Butch."

She couldn't help it. She laughed.

"You find that funny?" He lifted a dark eyebrow.

"No. Yes…you see, we call my dad Buck."

The little bit of conversation seemed to relieve the tension and he sank down by her. "Who are you?"

She took a moment, then said, "I'm a private investigator."

He looked at her with a startled expression. "Are you investigating me?"

"Yes."

Brodie was taken aback. He'd never met a detective who looked quite like her before, with soft brown eyes, high cheekbones and a bow of a mouth. A kissable, tantalizing mouth. Her blond hair was pulled back like the other day, but today she wore snug-fitting jeans and a knit top. She appeared more like a model than a detective.

He swallowed. "Why?"

"It's kind of hard to explain."

He thought for a minute. She took his comb, which probably had strands of his hair on it. Oh no. He jumped to his feet. "Were you trying to get my DNA?"

Her eyes grew big, as if she didn't quite expect him to grasp that so quickly. "Yes."

"Who is it?"

She frowned. "What?"

"I assume some woman I've slept with is trying to find out if I'm the father of her child. Who is it?" Just saying the words caused a painful knot to form in his stomach. He was always careful, always used protection, but there was always that slim chance.

She shook her head. "It's nothing like that."

He removed his hat and wiped his forehead with the sleeve of his shirt. "Then what is it?" Relief oozed out of him. He could actually feel it.

"Do you know a Helen Braxton?"

"No. Never heard the name. Who is she?"

There was silence for a moment.

Alex took her time, not knowing quite how to do this. The paternity thing threw her and she wondered just how many women there'd been in his life. Probably more than he could remember. His relief was very evident. She was getting sidetracked and she brought her thoughts back to his question.

There wasn't an easy way to do this so she just came out with it. "Someone stole her baby from the hospital nursery almost forty years ago."

The dark eyebrow rose again. "So? What does that have to do with me?"

She stared at him. "She thinks you might be her son."

He drew back. "You're joking, right?"

"No." She held his gaze.

An eerie quiet wrapped around them. A cow mooed, the dogs barked in response and trotted to the corral to investigate. The hot sun fueled an unbearable heat. A typical summer day, but there was nothing typical about the innuendoes and unspoken truths.

He studied his hat in his hand. "Why does she think I'm her son?"

"She saw your picture in the paper and you resemble her other sons."

"That's it?" His face creased into a frown. "You invade my privacy because this woman *thinks* I *might* be her long lost son. You have no proof. Nothing."

"No. That's why I wanted to do this discreetly, to keep you from ever knowing—if it wasn't true."

"How noble of you."

"I realize the lady has been grieving for a long time and that she's grasping at straws, but there is something very similar about all the photos she showed me."

"Get off my ranch, Ms. Donovan. I don't want to hear any more of this nonsense."

She stood, knowing this conversation was over. He was getting angry.

"And I want my damn comb back."

She reached into her back pocket and pulled it out. "The lab couldn't get a clear DNA. They would need your blood or saliva." She held up a hand as he made to speak. "If you're curious, here's my card." She fished it out of her front pocket. "Just call me."

"I'm not remotely curious. I know exactly who my parents are. My father was in Germany when I was born, but my aunt was with my mother and took care of us until we flew to Germany to be with my dad. No mystery at all. You have the wrong man."

She chewed on the inside of her lip. "The resemblance between you and the Braxtons is too big a coincidence to ignore." She paused. "The Braxtons have back hair and blue eyes—just like you."

"You have the wrong man, Ms. Donovan," he repeated, not even blinking.

She held his gaze. "Prove it."

He sucked in a breath at her audacity. "I know who my parents are. Believe me, there were times when I wished they weren't, as all kids do, but I'm stuck with them. My father had black hair and blue eyes. It's not indigenous to one family."

"A simple little test, Mr. Hayes, could ease Mrs. Braxton's mind. After all these years she's still desperate to find her son. I just want to help her, and hopefully, it won't be at your expense."

"I see no need for a test. I'm not her son."

"If you change your mind, you have my card." She

headed for her car, then swung back. "I'm sorry about the comb."

He didn't answer and she made her way back to the city. She didn't call Mrs. Braxton. She decided to give Brodie some time. It was a very complicated situation and Alex knew she was being pulled more and more into it.

She couldn't shake that feeling growing inside her— that Brodie was wrong.

BRODIE TOSSED AND TURNED, unable to get Alex Donovan out of his mind. An investigator—that was the last thing he'd expected. But he knew from the start that she wasn't a girl out for a good time. She was out to destroy his life.

Not her exactly, but her client. And just because he had black hair and blue eyes! He knew who he was. There were no doubts about that. He sat up in bed as something occurred to him. Alex had said the woman was desperate. What if Mrs. Braxton tried to contact his mother? She'd found him so there would be no problem in finding his mother. In Claudia's fragile health that could be disastrous.

He had to make sure that never happened.

In the morning he drove into Dallas to find Alex Donovan. If a simple test would keep Mrs. Braxton away from his mother, then he'd do it. He didn't want someone continually hounding his mother or him.

He found the office without a problem. It was a small building that housed several businesses. Donovan Investigations was on the bottom floor and the door was open. Workmen were going in and out. He was about to leave when he saw her talking to one of the guys.

He watched her for a moment. She talked with her hands and her face was animated. He felt a hitch in his throat. From the first moment he set eyes on her, he knew she was different. His instincts were right on target. He just wished his heart didn't do a dog paddle when he looked at her.

Surprise filtered across her face when she noticed him.

"Mr. Hayes." She walked to him, her hips moving with an easy tantalizing rhythm.

"I've decided to take the test." He came right to the point, ignoring that sparkle in her eyes.

"Oh. Sure. I'll set it up and I'll get a card with the address." She hurried into an office and came back with a business card in her hand.

"Thank you for doing this," she said, handing it to him. "Mrs. Braxton will be very grateful."

"I'm not doing this for Mrs. Braxton." He wanted to make that very clear. "I figured if she found me she could easily find my mother, who is not in the best of health. I will not have her harassed by an insane woman who thinks I'm her long lost son."

"Mrs. Braxton might be desperate, but she wouldn't do that."

"Yeah. Like you wouldn't enter my home under false pretences and steal to get my DNA. I want to stop this now before my mother gets involved."

"The reason I did that was so you wouldn't have to know. I am sorry."

Those brown eyes begged him to understand, but he turned away. "There's no need to contact me after this. Just give Mrs. Braxton the results and we're done."

"Mr. Hayes…"

He swung back to her. "That's it, Ms. Donovan. I don't want to see you again."

Chapter Four

Brodie had lunch with Cleo and his mother. Although he tried to push the DNA test from his mind, it kept nagging at him. He wondered why Mrs. Braxton thought he was her son. Maybe she wasn't stable, and looked for her son in every black-haired, blue-eyed man she saw.

Claudia went to lie down for a nap. Brodie helped Cleo take the dishes to the kitchen.

"Great chicken-fried steak, Cleo."

"You're easy to please. Claudie's so picky."

Brodie leaned against the cabinet as Cleo methodically stacked the plates side by side in the dishwasher and slipped the silverware into the slots. "Mother and I have been talking about when I was kid," he said matter-of-factly. "You were with my mother when I born, right?" He hadn't anticipated asking his aunt this question. The words just slipped out of their own volition.

She glanced up for a brief second. "Sure was. I was separated from husband number two and Claudie called wanting to stay with me while she had her baby.

Tom was on some sort of special assignment in Germany and couldn't leave, but he wanted you born in the States."

Brodie folded his arms across his chest as more questions filled his mind. "Were you in the room with her?"

Cleo put soap in the dispenser and closed the door. "Yes. You know how your mother's afraid of being alone. I stood right by her side, holding her hand as you came into the world. Tom was on the phone and I was talking to him while trying to soothe Claudie. Tom was so happy when I told him it was a boy."

The knot in his gut eased. "Mother didn't stay in Dallas long after that, did she?"

"Good heavens, no. She couldn't wait for Tom to see you. You had a thatch of black hair and beautiful blue eyes just like your father." Cleo wiped her hands on a dishtowel. "You must have been a week old when Claudie flew to Germany. When I talked to her later, she said Tom was enthralled with you."

Brodie made a face. "But not so much as I grew older."

"Sweetie, he was disappointed you were so hell-bent on the rodeo, but that doesn't mean he wasn't proud."

"Sometimes I'm not so sure about that."

Cleo clicked her tongue. "Come with me. I want to show you something." He followed her into the den. She opened a cabinet and pulled out a photo album. "Take a look at this."

He sat on the sofa and flipped through the album in awe. There were newspaper clippings of his rodeo triumphs through the years. His parents had kept track of his life—his successes. For a moment he was speechless.

"Tom was never good at showing his feelings, but you were his son and he was proud of you."

He touched a clipping from the national finals in Vegas. "He'd told me that in Vegas, but I thought they were just words he felt he had to say."

"Brodie, both your parents love you." She eyed him for a moment. "Why are you thinking of all this now?"

He closed the album. "As I said, Mother and I have been doing a lot of talking and I was wondering how our lives got so out of control that I had to leave to make my own way in the world."

"Tom, God rest his soul, was a hard man. He believed his way was the right way and he didn't leave you many choices."

"Yeah. I guess I was as hard and stubborn as he was."

"Mmm." She carried the album back to the cabinet. "I'm glad you and Claudie are getting along better now."

"Me, too." And he meant that. All the years of estrangement had certainly strained their relationship—there would always be some tension between them. But he was now able to talk to his mother without his stomach coiling into knots. At least sometimes.

"They love you. Never doubt that."

He nodded. Part of him finally believed that.

"Now we just have to find a woman to love you."

He grinned. "I can find plenty of those."

"Brodie Hayes, you bad boy." Cleo wagged a finger at him. "I mean a forever kind of love that produces babies and happiness."

All of a sudden he saw Alex Donovan's face, her soft brown eyes and kissable mouth.

"Do you think there's such a thing as real happiness?"

"Heavens. Don't ask me. I certainly never found it, and believe me I tried. But you, with that face, that dimple and those gorgeous eyes—a woman is just waiting to worship at your feet."

His mouth twitched. "Not exactly what I had in mind." He stood. "I'll head back to the ranch. Tell Mother I'll call her later."

Cleo studied him, her eyes narrowed. "You know Melvin has a friend who has a niece...."

"No. No blind dates." He reached for his hat.

"Suit yourself, cowboy."

Brodie left feeling much better. He never realized he had a germ of doubt about the DNA test, but after talking to Cleo it was gone. He was not Helen Braxton's son.

TWO WEEKS LATER Alex sat at her desk looking at the DNA results. Ninety-nine point nine. Brodie Hayes was Helen Braxton's biological son. She took a moment for that to sink in while she ran her sweaty palms down the thighs of her jeans. How did she tell Brodie this kind of news? For she knew she had to tell him first.

Mrs. Braxton and her family were going to be ecstatic, but it was going to tear apart Brodie's world. Could she do that? For a brief second she had an urge to let sleeping dogs lie. This was going to hurt so many people, especially Brodie.

Alex had been hired by the Braxtons and she shouldn't even be thinking about Brodie and his feelings. She was human, though, and this wasn't going to be easy on anyone.

There were so many unanswered questions—like how Travis Braxton ended up with the Hayes family? Where was the real Brodie Hayes? As a detective she wanted to delve deeper to find the truth, but right now all she could think was that this news was going to shatter Brodie.

BRODIE TWIRLED THE ROPE over his head and sailed it deftly toward a post. It landed squarely over its mark and he yanked the rope tight.

"Wow," Joey Henshaw said. Joey'd been bitten with the rodeo bug. During the summer, the young boy who lived on a neighboring ranch helped Brodie keep the Cowboy Up running. He was full of questions about the rodeo and eager to learn as much as he could.

Brodie remembered that feeling of being full of dreams and hopes, of being ten feet tall and bulletproof. There was nothing he couldn't do. The world was his rodeo.

But what happened when the dream was accomplished? What happened after the victory? Where was the happiness? Shouldn't that be his reward for surviving and beating the odds in such a grueling, competitive sport? He felt there had to be more to life than just living day-to-day.

But he'd done things his way against his parents' objections. He had to win. There was no other recourse for him. He'd had to prove himself, not to his parents, but for his own satisfaction and happiness.

As Joey swung the rope above his head and aimed for the post, Brodie wondered if he was still trying to do that. To prove to himself he'd been right in the decisions he'd made. That was important to his peace of mind.

"Look, Brodie," Joey shouted. "I roped it. If I keep

practicing, maybe I can get as good as you, Colter Kincaid and Tripp Daniels."

"That's a big dream, kid."

"I know." Joey kicked at the dirt with his boot. "Tripp does magic with the rope. He can make it go exactly where he wants it to. And, Colter, he's just great."

"It takes a lot of practice." Brodie remembered all the days they'd practiced, over and over. Three cowboys bound by friendship, determined to make a success of their lives. They all roped, but it was clear early on that Tripp and Colter were the more talented in that area. To win, their timing had to be perfect. Brodie's forte was riding the big bulls.

"But I'll never be able to ride a bull like you."

Brodie jerked Joey's hat low. "That takes guts, practice and a little insanity."

Joey grinned. "I got guts and my sister says I'm crazy."

They stopped talking as plumes of dust headed their way. Amidst the cloud was a Jeep. *Alex Donovan.* What the hell did she want?

"That's it for the day, kid. Your dad probably has chores for you to do."

"Yeah. See you tomorrow." Joey swung over the fence, grabbed the reins of his horse and galloped away across the pastures to his parents' ranch.

The Jeep rolled steadily toward the corrals. He didn't want to think about what this visit meant. He just wanted to get rid of her.

She stepped out in tight-fitting jeans. A white tank top outlined her full breasts. The sun glistened off her blond hair and kissed her long arms and slim neck. Her pale olive skin contrasted deeply with her hair. It drew his eyes like a magnet. He didn't take any pleasure in that reaction.

This woman was bad news. Real bad news.

She climbed the fence. "Mr. Hayes, may I speak with you, please?"

He picked up the rope from the ground, taking his time looping it into a circle. After that, he placed it on the post and slowly walked toward her.

"Ms. Donovan, you and I have nothing to say to one another. I thought I made that very clear."

"You did, and I'm sorry, but I have to speak with you."

That anxious tone in her voice curled his stomach muscles into a tight rope of pain. Years ago he had that same reaction when he was about to ride a bull that was known to be meaner than the devil. Just like back then, he took a deep breath and was ready to face whatever he had to.

He walked to the gate and met her by the bench under the oak tree. Without a word she handed him a piece of paper.

"I don't know how else to do this, but that's the DNA results." She paused. "You're Helen Braxton's biological son."

Without looking at the paper, he handed it back to her. "There has to be a mistake. I spoke with my aunt and she was with my mother when I was born. She never left her side until my mother boarded a plane with me for Germany to be with my father. I'm not sure what's going on here, but you have the wrong man. I resent this intrusion into my life."

"I deeply apologize, but DNA doesn't lie."

He whipped off his hat and slapped it against his leg. "Lady, just stay out of my life." He swung toward the corrals.

"You know something's not right or you wouldn't have asked about your birth."

Her words stopped him in his tracks. "Go away and leave me in peace."

"I'm sorry, but I can't do that. Travis Braxton was born five days after you in the same hospital and—"

He glared at her. "That means nothing. My mother had taken me home by then."

"There's a connection, Mr. Hayes. I feel it and so do you. Don't you want to know the truth?"

"No."

"You're lying. You're a fighter, a survivor and you're not going to rest until you know what happened all those years ago."

"You don't know anything about me."

"I know enough."

He sucked in a breath that felt as hot as the sun that seared his skin. "Please leave." He took a couple of steps and turned, his eyes catching hers. "Have you told the Braxtons?"

"No. I thought you deserved to know first."

"Thank you."

"You're welcome. I know this has to be a shock."

"You don't know the half of it. I'll be forty in October and you're telling me that my whole life has been a lie. There's some mistake. I want the test done again."

"Sure. I don't blame you."

That concerned look in her eyes threw him. Why did she care about him? He wasn't her client.

"And I'd like to talk to my aunt again just to clear up any misunderstandings."

"Sure."

"And I'd rather Helen Braxton not know until after the second test."

"Okay."

He lifted an eyebrow. "You're being very agreeable."

"I want to make this as easy as possible on everyone."

"Why do you care, lady?"

She shrugged. "Like I said, I know it has to be traumatic to have your world turned upside down."

"Are you talking from experience?"

A smile flashed across her face. "My world is always upside down. I seem to be hanging on by my fingernails."

"To me, you look like a lady who can cope." His eyes met hers and he realized they were flirting, getting personal—something he didn't want to do.

"I'm a Donovan. I'm supposed to have grit in my backbone, and in some other places, too. My father wanted a boy and he got a girl, so I've been conditioned to cope with just about anything."

"Could you cope with finding out that you're not a Donovan?"

She grimaced. "That would be upsetting, and I can empathize with you."

"Don't," he said. "When the second test is done, we'll have the truth."

She laid the paper on the bench and the summer breeze ruffled the blond strands around her face.

Quickly brushing them back she said, "I'll leave this copy with you. You might want to read it. It's ninety-nine point nine. You *are* Helen Braxton's son."

He clenched his jaw.

She hesitated. "Would you like to know something about the Braxton family?"

"No."

She inclined her head. "Fine. I'll call the lab and you can go in when you want." He didn't respond and she stared at him for a moment, then walked to her car.

As he watched her drive away, he sank down on the bench. He glanced down at the paper beside him. Ninety-nine point nine. How could that be?

Staring off into the distance, he saw cattle walking down the fence row to a water trough. He knew everything about each cow, who he'd bought her from, how old she was, how many calves she'd produced and when the calf was sold. He knew everything about his cows and his horses, but it seemed he knew very little about his own family.

He always thought he knew who he was. No matter what these test results said, he knew he was a cowboy right down to his soul. Even though he had different goals for himself than the ones laid out by his parents that didn't mean they weren't connected. Tom and Claudia Hayes were his parents.

Squeezing his eyes shut, he felt the red orbs of the sun sting behind his eyelids. Could the DNA be correct? Could he be someone other than Brodie Hayes? For the first time he let himself think about that possibility.

Opening his eyes, he removed his hat and wiped the sweat from his brow. Alex was right. He had to know the truth.

FORTY-FIVE MINUTES LATER he walked through his mother's front door. He found Cleo in the kitchen making dinner.

She glanced up from the stove. "Brodie, I didn't know you were coming this evening."

He took a seat on the rattan barstool and forced himself to relax. "I didn't plan on it, but I thought I'd stop in to see how Mother's doing."

"She's much better. She's out playing bridge with her uppity friends."

"That's good. At least she's getting out. I was going to talk to the doctor about her going through some depression."

"Claudie's not depressed. In her fragile state she's used to attention, especially from me. If I coddle her, she's right as rain."

Brodie thought that was probably true. His mother had always needed lots of attention. She depended on Cleo. But that wasn't what he wanted to talk about. He wanted to talk about his birth and found it difficult to bring up the subject.

"What are you cooking?" he asked instead.

"I made a fruit salad and a green salad and I'm grilling a chicken breast to go with it. I try to cook healthy for Claudie."

"You take very good care of her."

"Always have. When she was diagnosed with rheumatic fever as a kid, she couldn't run and play and I felt bad."

"So you made up for it by pampering her?"

"Sometimes. Other times she makes me so mad I want to strangle her, but she knows I'll do anything for her."

Brodie shifted uneasily on the stool. What would Cleo do for Claudia? Where would she draw the line? He didn't like the thoughts running through his head. Time for some answers.

"I asked about my birth earlier, but I'd like to talk about it again."

Cleo put the salads in the refrigerator. "Okay. What do you want to know?"

"You said you were with my mother when I was born."

"Never left her side."

"After you brought us home, we stayed with you until I was a week old, then you took us to the airport and saw us onto the plane?"

Cleo closed the refrigerator. "Not exactly."

"What do you mean?"

"The night before Claudia was scheduled to fly out, Harold, my husband, called and wanted to meet and talk. I wanted to see him, too, hoping we could put our marriage back together. Claudia said to go; that she'd catch a cab in the morning to the airport and that's what she did. She called later to let me know she'd arrived safely." Cleo's eyes narrowed. "Why are you asking all these questions?"

Brodie didn't know how to answer that, so he pulled the DNA test results from his pocket, walked around the bar and laid them on the counter in front of her.

"What's that?"

He took a breath. "It's a DNA test saying I'm Helen Braxton's biological son."

"What!"

"Read the paper."

She quickly scanned it. "Who's Helen Braxton?"

"Her son was born five days after me in the same hospital. He was stolen from the nursery."

"And she thinks you're that son?"

"Yes. And the DNA test says I am."

"That's ridiculous." Cleo shook her head. "If you're supposed to be this woman's son, where is the real Brodie Hayes?"

"I don't know. It's all very confusing."

"It has to be some kind of scam or something because I was there when Claudie gave birth. We brought you home."

"It doesn't make any sense. That's why I'm taking another test."

"Good, that will solve this." She turned toward the stove and Brodie caught her forearms, staring into her eyes.

"Tell me that I'm Tom and Claudia's son." He couldn't keep that desperate plea out of his voice.

"Brodie, for heaven's sakes, you are. I wouldn't lie to you."

He knew his aunt well enough to know she was telling the truth. He released her arms and swallowed hard. "I don't understand any of this."

"I don't, either, but something's not right. Why are these people trying to destroy your life and Cla...ohmygosh."

In a panic, Cleo slapped her face with the palms of both her hands. "You can't let Claudie find out anything about this. It will upset her terribly and she could have a heart attack."

"Don't worry. I don't plan on telling her anything until another lab runs the test." Now that he thought about it, he wasn't going back to the same lab. To make sure everything was on the up-and-up, he'd prefer a lab Ms. Donovan didn't do business with on a regular basis. And he intended to let her know as soon as possible.

Chapter Five

When Alex pulled into her spot at the office the next morning, Brodie's truck was in the parking lot. Her heart hammered against her ribs. All night she'd thought about him and what he must be going through. She wondered if his presence here this morning meant that he was ready to face the truth.

For someone so tough and fearless this sudden twist in his life had to be upsetting. She felt bad this was causing him so much pain. The last thing she wanted was to hurt him, but she couldn't stop that now.

Grabbing her purse and briefcase, she got out. Brodie immediately swung his truck door open and walked toward her in his loose-limbed way. Without a word, he handed her a business card.

"That's the name and location of a lab. They will do another DNA test. If you'd inform Mrs. Braxton, I'd appreciate it."

"You want the test done at another lab?"

"Yes. To keep everything on the up-and-up."

"Oh."

"Nothing against you personally, but this is my life and I would prefer to use a lab that does not do business with you regularly."

"Okay." She respected his decision and the care he was taking with this. "I'll let Mrs. Braxton know."

"The lab will notify me, so we don't have to have contact with each other."

She looked up at him. "But I do insist on being notified of the results."

"Of course."

She squinted against the morning sun. "What if the test is the same?"

"It won't be."

He was still in denial. When the truth finally hit him it was going to be twice as difficult. This cowboy was in for the biggest fall of his life.

Turning, he walked back to his truck and drove away.

In her office, she let out a deep breath, wondering what to do. How to tell Mrs. Braxton without breaking her word to Brodie? A good P.I. didn't straddle the fence, working both sides, unless it was for a very good reason. She considered this a good reason. Brodie needed time and she was going to give it to him.

Picking up the phone, she called Mrs. Braxton. "Helen, this is Alex. Brodie would rather the DNA test be done at a lab he's chosen. Could you please give another sample?" She read off the name and location.

"What's going on, Alex?"

"Brodie insists the lab not have any connection to Donovan Investigations. He's just staggered by the whole thing." She wanted to be as honest as possible.

"I can understand that." There was a pause. "Does this mean…"

"It means Brodie wants the DNA done on his terms. He's not happy with this intrusion into his life."

"Oh, my. I don't want to upset him."

"Helen, Brodie is already upset and it's only going to get worse. He's almost forty and secure in the life he's been living."

"My daughter tells me I should just let him be, but I can't. I…ah…"

Again Alex felt this woman's pain. "We'll have the results soon and we'll take it from there."

"Okay. I'll do the test today."

"Thanks. I'll be in touch."

Now they would wait. But Alex already knew the results. So did Brodie. This gave him time, though. Time to adjust. Time to accept the unbelievable.

NADDY WON fifteen hundred dollars on the slot machines and she and Ethel were staying a few days longer in Vegas. Alex knew better than to try and dissuade her. When she returned, Alex knew she wouldn't have a dime of the money left. Naddy believed in living every day as if it were her last.

Alex and Buck worked on the new cases. Valerie Cryder was accused of killing her husband and two children. The DA hired them to go the extra mile on Mrs. Cryder's life, digging through all the dirty laundry, so to speak. Buck was handling most of it.

She had two other cases going that took up a lot of her time—a woman who was allegedly cheating on her husband, and a man who might be fooling around on his wife.

Sometimes she didn't understand why people got married—so much cheating and divorce. Everyone was looking for the same thing—happiness. It seemed a very elusive thing for most people.

She had the potential husband-cheater's routine down. He worked for a large insurance company. He left the building every day at five minutes after five. He drove to a local bar and ordered bourbon and water. After one drink, he left the bar and went home. On those nights he worked late, he was actually working. In Alex's experience, this situation was very rare. Most of the time the wife's instincts were correct. Alex gave the wife her findings and she didn't believe it. So Alex was still watching him.

The other case was a different situation. The wife met a man three times a week at a motel in plain sight. Alex always hated to reveal this kind of information, especially when children were involved. But it was what she was paid to do.

At the end of the week she helped Buck on the Cryder case. While she worked, Brodie was never far from her mind. Every day she waited for the lab to call and confirm the results. She was still waiting.

BRODIE UNSADDLED Jax and rubbed him down. In the heat he didn't like to overwork him, but he'd spent most of the afternoon riding a fence line checking for a break. He checked his fences regularly because cows were known to perceive that the grass was always greener on the other side of the fence. They'd put their heads through the barbed wire and push until they could munch on his neighbor's grass. Sometimes the older wire broke and he didn't want his cattle straying onto his neighbor's property.

He was glad he was busy. He didn't want to think.

He led Jax into the corral and removed his bridle. The horse followed him, nuzzling his back as he poured horse feed into a trough. Gobbling the feed, Jax raised his head and neighed.

"You're welcome," Brodie said as if he understood what the neighing meant. And he felt pretty sure he did.

Butch and Buck drank thirstily from the water trough. "Come on, guys. I'll feed you, too."

The dogs followed him as he made his way to the house. Before he reached it, his cell rang. He saw the number—the lab. He took a deep breath before he clicked on.

An hour later he sat in his truck in front of the lab with the results in his hand. *Ninety-nine point nine*. That didn't leave any room for error. That's what the lab technician had told him. He was Helen Braxton's biological son.

He drew in a breath that felt like a fishbone going down his throat—sharp, jagged and painful. Tom and Claudia Hayes weren't his parents. He wasn't Brodie Hayes, their son.

The truth of that finally sunk in and so many conflicting emotions tore at him. What had happened all those years ago? How did Helen Braxton's baby end up with Claudia Hayes?

Numbly, he gazed out at the summer day. The sky was a brilliant blue and a lone oak tree took pride of place in a small courtyard to the side of the clinic. A woman and two kids sat there on a stone bench, probably waiting for someone in the twelve-story building. He saw them, but he didn't see them. All his thoughts were chaotic and disturbed. He was at the crossroads of his life and what he did now would set the pattern for the years ahead. Of those two things he was certain.

He ran his hand over the steering wheel and hit it with his fist. Damn it all to hell. He wouldn't let this rip him apart. He was stronger than that. He'd survived a bull throwing him against a fence, leaving him with cracked ribs and a broken collarbone. He'd survived several concussions and broken bones and he'd survive this.

Starting the engine, he thought about Colter and Tripp. They survived heartache, pain and family tragedy and so would he. Since Colter was out of town, he thought about calling Tripp, but he wasn't that weak. He could handle this alone. The first order of business was confronting his mother.

All the way to her house he kept thinking he had to handle the matter with the utmost care. In his mother's fragile health, he had to approach the subject very delicately. But he needed answers and he had to get them.

WHEN HE ARRIVED, Cleo and his mother were eating dinner.

"Brodie, darling," Claudia said, smiling. "What a pleasant surprise. Have you had dinner?"

"No. I'm not hungry, but I'll take a glass of tea."

Cleo stood, her eyes on Brodie. The message was clear—don't upset your mother.

"How have you been?" he asked, taking a seat and removing his hat.

"Much better. I've started playing bridge again."

"That's good. You need to get out more."

Cleo set the glass in front of him, her eyes watching him like a hawk. He ignored her.

"Did you stop by for a reason, darling?"

"Yes. I'd like to talk about something."

Cleo cleared her throat rather loudly.

"Are you okay?" Claudia asked, staring at Cleo.

"Yes. I just don't want you to get upset."

"Upset? Why would I get upset talking to my son?" Claudia glanced from him to Cleo. "Do you know what Brodie wants to talk about?"

"I'm not sure," Cleo replied.

"Mother, do you know Helen Braxton?"

Claudia thought for a minute. "No. The name doesn't sound familiar."

"Brodie…"

Brodie held up a hand, stopping Cleo.

"I am your son. I believe that."

Claudia's eyes narrowed. "Of course you are."

He pulled the DNA results from his pocket and unfolded it. "I'm going to show you something and I want you to stay calm. We can talk about this. Okay?"

"Okay."

He laid the paper in front of her and saw that his hand shook slightly. His hands never shook, not even when he'd ridden El Diablo. He swallowed hard, forcing down his weakness. "This paper says that I'm Helen Braxton's biological son."

"Don't be ridiculous." Claudia brushed the paper away with a nervous laugh.

"I thought it was insane at first, too. But I've taken two DNA tests."

"You are Tom's son. Go look at your father's picture. You look just like him."

"I know, but DNA doesn't lie."

"In this case it does." Claudia rose to her feet. "I don't know why this Helen person is trying to steal my son, but she has the wrong man. You are Brodie Hayes."

"Mother…"

"I don't care what that test says. You're my son. I gave birth to you. I'm not talking about this anymore." Without another word, she walked to her room and quietly closed the door.

Cleo lifted an eyebrow. "She took that very well."

"A little too well," Brodie said. And he didn't know what to make of it. He expected anger and resentment, not calmness.

"Just forget about that Braxton woman," Cleo suggested. "You're not a baby anymore."

"I know, but someone stole Helen Braxton's baby from the nursery. How did that baby end up with Claudia?"

"I don't believe it."

Brodie tapped the DNA papers. "This says otherwise."

Cleo shrugged. "None of this makes any sense."

"Yes, especially since Travis Braxton was born five days after me. There was no way the babies could have been switched in the nursery. That wouldn't make any sense since the Braxtons' baby was missing and the Hayes baby had already gone home."

"As I said, just forget about it."

He reached for his hat. "Sorry. I can't do that."

"Brodie…"

He wasn't listening. He was already out the door.

WHEN ALEX GOT THE RESULTS, her first thought was Brodie. How was he taking it? She felt responsible for the whole mess, even though she was only doing a job. Mrs. Braxton had already found Brodie and if Alex had turned down the case, another investigator would have taken it. Maybe Buck was right and she was too soft-hearted.

She would give Brodie time before she contacted him. By tomorrow she had to let Helen know. She couldn't put it off any longer.

Buck walked into her office. "You did a great job sniffing out info at the beauty shop and the spa on the Cryder woman. She's a fine piece of work."

Was that praise? She could hardly believe her ears. She flexed her fingers. "It's amazing the information you can get while getting your nails done."

"I'm going to put a steak on the grill tonight. You going to be home?"

"Yeah," she replied, surprised at this offer. They usually did their own thing.

"I'll put another steak on. See you at home."

She wondered if the heat was getting to him. He didn't seem like Buck at all.

Later, at home, she made a salad to go with the steak

and baked potatoes. Buck wouldn't touch the salad, but she liked it.

Cutting into her steak, she asked, "What do you think makes women like Mrs. Cryder commit such a heinous crime?"

"Greed." He dumped Tabasco sauce on his meat. He put it on everything, even his eggs. "She found a rich man and decided to get rid of her family. If the police had believed it was a robbery gone bad, she would have gotten away with it."

"People do strange things sometimes in the name of love."

"It's greed and selfishness, not love."

She wouldn't debate that. She was just glad they were talking. On a whim she decided to share the Braxton case with him.

"You remember the missing baby case I was working?"

"Sure. A waste of time," he replied around a mouthful of food.

"No, it wasn't. The man Mrs. Braxton believed was her son really is her biological son."

He stopped chewing. "You got to be kidding."

"No."

Buck took a swallow of his beer. "How old is this man?"

"He'll be forty in October."

"Why in the hell does the Braxton woman want to tear apart his life now?"

Alex was taken aback by this reaction. "Because someone stole her baby and she has to know that he's alive and well."

"Doesn't she realize what she's doing to his life?"

"Buck," she said, trying to reason with him, "losing a baby is a traumatic thing, something a woman never gets over. Even though Mrs. Braxton was able to go on with her life, her missing son was always at the back of her mind. That's why Brodie Hayes's photo in the paper triggered her hope again. She's lost two other sons. Brodie is her only living boy. The need to see him is never going away."

"You women have all these emotions that us men just aren't equipped with. We look at the facts. Once you get the emotions involved everything goes to hell."

"I get involved. I admit that. I'm more sensitive than I should be for a cop or a private investigator."

He pointed his knife at her. "You get that from your mother."

They never talked about Joan and she welcomed this opportunity. "My mother was sensitive and caring?"

"Damn right. Waterworks was a regular display and when it was that time of the month, hell, I stayed out of the house."

"Did you ever hold her and tell her you understood?"

His eyebrows knotted together like a rope. "Hell, no, 'cause I didn't understand why every little thing made her cry."

"What did she cry about?" She might be pressing her luck, but she wanted to hear more.

"When I didn't call and tell her I was going to be late. I was a cop and couldn't call her every few minutes. She cried when I forgot her birthday, and the waterworks lasted a week when I forgot our anniversary."

"She had reasons to cry. That's just plain insensitive."

"But that's me, girl, and you know it. Your mother knew it, too, when she married me. Don't know why she wanted me to be someone I wasn't. Don't know what she saw in me in the first place, but I was so crazy about her that it didn't matter. She was different than I was. Maybe that's why I fell for her. She was this gentle, soft-spoken woman who never saw the bad in anyone."

"Maybe she saw some good in you."

"Could be, but she had to look hard for it."

Her heart filled with joy at this wonderful glimpse of her mother. Alex had heard precious little about her all these years.

"You never talk about her."

He shrugged.

"A man thing, huh?"

"You got it. Talking is a woman thing." He took another swallow of his beer. "Speaking of women— when the hell is Naddy coming back?"

"When she runs out of money."

"God. I shouldn't have to raise my mother."

"Naddy can take care of herself. You told me that."

"Mmm."

There was silence for a moment and it wasn't uncomfortable like in the past. That easy companionship felt surreal since she'd wished for it so many times as a kid.

"So how did Mrs. Braxton take the news that this Brodie Hayes is her son?"

Alex laid her fork down. Back to business. "I haven't told her yet."

"Why?"

"I'm giving Brodie time to accept the situation."

His eyes narrowed. "Brodie? Are you involved with this man?"

She met his eyes squarely. "By involved do you mean attracted to, sleeping with or generally making a fool of myself?"

"All of the above," he snapped.

"I just feel this man's pain. That's all."

"Good grief, you're just like Joan. Get your head on straight. We run an investigating agency and our clients put a lot of trust in us. Mrs. Braxton is our client and she is your first priority. Get on that phone and call her this instant."

She slowly stood, throwing her napkin onto her plate. "This is my case and I will handle it my way." She gritted her teeth and counted to three. "A lot of lives will be changed when the DNA results are revealed so I'm taking it slow. If you have a problem with that, you can take me off the payroll."

"Now you listen here…"

Alex grabbed her purse and headed for the door. So much for a nice evening. Buck had turned into his usual controlling, manipulative… No wonder her mother cried a lot. She felt like crying now. But she wouldn't.

She jumped into her Jeep and sat for a moment. How could one man make her doubt every decision she'd ever made? Buck wasn't getting to her this time. She'd made the right decision concerning Brodie and Mrs. Braxton.

As she backed out of the driveway, she wondered how Brodie was taking the news of the second test. Pulling to the curb, she poked out his number. No answer. He either wasn't home or not taking calls. She had to tell him she was informing Mrs. Braxton in the morning of the DNA findings so she headed for the freeway and Mesquite.

Chapter Six

When Alex drove up to Brodie's ranch, everything was in darkness except for a couple of spotlights at the corrals. Through the beams of the light, she saw the dogs running toward the Jeep. She got out.

"Hey, guys, where's your master?"

One of the dogs barked and she had no idea if it was Buck or Butch. Since he was the mouthy one she decided it was Buck. Sensing she wasn't a danger or threat they trotted back to the barn.

She breathed in the fresh country air. A coyote howled in the distance and an owl hooted. She wasn't used to living in the country. The hum of traffic, horns honking and curse words hurled through the air were the usual night sounds in her world. But here was a peacefulness as comforting and pleasant as a hug from an old friend. She liked Brodie's ranch.

Her thoughts came back to him. Where was Brodie? He'd gotten the report so what would a stubborn hard-headed cowboy do?

Go home to confront his mother. She crawled back

into the Jeep and reached for a phone book she kept in the backseat. Actually, she had several books for different towns around Dallas. They were very useful for finding people and places quickly. Flipping through it she found Claudia Hayes's name and her address. Great. She knew the street. It was in a subdivision not too far away.

Thirty minutes later she drove by the house. Lights were on and the garage door was closed. No big white truck in sight. She drove by once again to make sure she hadn't missed it. Brodie wasn't there.

She wasn't sure why she had to find him tonight, but she was compelled to confront him. The second test had to have hit him like a ton of bricks. Where would he go to nurse his wounds? Where would a cowboy go when he was down?

A bar. A honky-tonk, good-time bar.

She grabbed the phone book again. There were several places in Fort Worth where cowboys hung out, but she was betting that Brodie hadn't gone that far. Stopping for a light, she thumbed to the yellow pages and ran her eyes down the list of nightclubs and bars. Good grief. This could take days.

How could she cut down the list? Reaching for her cell phone, she poked out a number.

"Hey, Dudley, this is Alex."

"Hey there, good-looking. What can I do you for?"

Dudley was one of her information sources. He knew everything there was to know about Dallas and Fort Worth, including some things he shouldn't know.

"I'm looking for a bar or nightclub in Dallas where cowboys hang out."

"Ah, honey, those cowboys'll do you in. They love their horses more than they'll ever love a woman."

"Don't be asinine. This is business."

"Mmm. You got a pencil and paper?"

Alex dug in her purse, turned a corner and pulled to the curb. Dudley spouted out several clubs and she marked them in the book.

"Thanks, Dud."

"Now, honey, if you want a good ride, look no further than Dud the man."

"You just never give up." Alex laughed. Dudley was her father's age, but he was always coming on to her. It was one of his quirky habits and she always ignored him.

"Not when there's a pretty lady involved."

"Good night, Dudley."

She heard his laugh as she clicked off.

BY THE TIME she found the fourth bar and Brodie's truck wasn't there, she was beginning to wonder if she had him pegged wrong. Maybe he wasn't licking his wounds. Maybe he had accepted the fact that DNA didn't lie.

That wasn't her impression of him, though. Brodie would not take this well. The fifth bar was Boots and Spurs and she drove around the block, looking for the truck. Bingo. There it was. Her instincts were right. Another truck backed out and she took the parking spot.

Now what? She could wait for him to come out or go in.

She slung her purse over her shoulder and got out, making sure her gun was within easy reach. Not that she planned on using it, but going into a bar alone after midnight was always a risk.

Opening the door, she stepped into the dimly lit, smoke-filled room. A Willie Nelson song played loudly on a jukebox and couples moved around the small dance floor, clinging to each other. Other couples sat at tables and booths. Several cowboys were bellied up to a horseshoe-shaped bar. Every cowboy had his hat on. Evidently drinking and dancing did not require a cowboy to remove his hat. She spotted Brodie at the end of the bar with a brunette leaning in close, talking to him.

She started to back out, but stopped. The brunette kissed his cheek and walked to a table. Alex weaved her way through the crowd to him. A cowboy stopped her.

"Hey, there, blondie. How about a dance?"

"No, thanks. I'm here to see someone." He followed her gaze to Brodie.

"You're out of luck, blondie. Brodie ain't in the mood tonight. Get my drift." He winked.

"Thanks for the information." She winked back and pushed past him to Brodie's left side. He didn't turn, just kept drinking a beer.

"Hi," she said.

"I told you I'm not…" His words trailed off as he saw who was talking to him.

"Well, if it ain't my favorite P.I."

"Could I speak with you, please?"

The music was so loud she wasn't sure if he'd answered or not, but from the look in his blue eyes she knew what his answer was.

"Another beer, Joe," Brodie said to the bartender. "And bring one for the lady."

"No, thanks," Alex quickly replied.

Brodie pushed back his hat and turned to her. "Lady, I figure I'm all done talking."

"This'll only take a minute."

"I don't have a minute." Brodie glanced at the bartender. "Joe, where's my damn beer?"

"Sorry, I'm not serving you anymore, Brodie. You've had enough. I suggest you get someone to drive you home."

"Hell, Joe, when did you get a conscience?"

"Go home, Brodie."

Brodie pulled his hat low over his eyes and strolled toward the door. He bumped into several people and they moved out of his way. Alex followed him out into the warm night air. Reaching into his pocket for his keys, Brodie stumbled into a truck. Alex knew she couldn't let him drive in his inebriated state.

When he managed to fish out the keys, she grabbed them.

"Hey. What do you think you're doing?"

"You're not driving in your condition."

"Like hell." He made a dive for the keys, tripped and fell against her. Under his weight she staggered backward into a vehicle, managing to keep them both upright. He was heavy, but something about his weight on her body and his musky male scent sent her senses into overdrive.

"God, I'm drunk," he mumbled, his breath fanning her hair.

"Yes, you are," she agreed. "Try to stand and I'll drive you home."

"You smell good—like ripe watermelon in the summertime." Not the most flattering of compliments, but his whiskey breath felt like a kiss on her heated skin.

"Try to stand," she said again, ignoring her feminine reaction.

He placed one hand on the truck and pushed upright.

She took his arm. "Come on. My Jeep's over here." Without one word of protest, he followed her. She opened the door and he slumped onto the seat, his feet still on the pavement.

"Brodie, put your feet inside," she said, but he didn't respond.

She picked up his boots and swung them around. Problem—his legs were too long and she couldn't wedge them in. Holding his legs with one hand, she reached for the seat-adjuster knob with the other. The seat slid back. She still had a problem.

"How long are your legs?"

He had a silly grin on his face and she wasn't sure he was conscious. Finally she managed to slide the boots inside. He then scooted up.

"Now you help."

He leaned his head against the head-rest and by his steady breathing she knew he was out cold. Leaving the door open, she ran back inside and told the bartender they were leaving Brodie's truck for the night.

Hurrying outside, she closed his door and jumped into the driver's seat. All the way to the ranch he never woke up. When they arrived, she drove as close to the back door as she could get. Getting him out of the Jeep and into the house was going to be another problem.

She opened his door and shook him. "Brodie, wake up. You're home." She did that three times before he stirred. "Stay awake," she said, pulling his feet out. "We have to walk to the door. Put your arm around my neck."

He drifted back to sleep.

"Brodie," she shouted.

He blinked.

"Try to stand and put your arm around my neck. And stay awake."

After a couple of attempts, he managed to get to his feet, his body swaying back and forth. She grabbed him and he gripped her around the neck. Slowly they made their way to the door.

It was locked. Damn. She heaved a deep breath and loosened her hold on him so she could dig in her pocket for his car keys, hoping his house key was on the ring. The dogs came to investigate, barking at a slumped Brodie.

"Hush," she said. Since it was dark she didn't have a clue what was a car key and what was a house key. Maintaining her hold on Brodie, she used the trial-and-error method. The first key wouldn't fit. The second worked. She felt like cheering.

Pushing the door wide, they half staggered and half walked inside. She kicked the door closed with her foot. The house was in total darkness and she had no idea where the light switches were.

Brodie's weight became heavier, as did his breathing. "Stay awake," she said, feeling on the wall for a switch. After several clumsy tries she found one and flipped it. Light lit up the breakfast room. After the darkness it took a while for her eyes to adjust, but now she could see where they were going.

They made the trek through the den, down a hall and into his bedroom. Moonlight streamed through the windows. She stopped by the side of the bed and turned him. As if sensing what she wanted him to do, he fell backward onto the bed.

Gulping in deep breaths, she rubbed her aching arms and stretched her tired back. This wasn't in her job description. She looked down at the sleeping cowboy. Now what? She couldn't leave him like this with his feet hanging off the bed.

Once again she picked up his boots and swung his legs around. Now his feet hung off the bed because he wasn't positioned correctly. There wasn't anything she could do about that. She stared down at his feet. He'd probably sleep better without his boots. How do you remove a cowboy's boots?

Mmm. Very carefully, she supposed.

With both hands, she grabbed a boot and pulled to no avail. Damn. Were they glued on? She placed her foot against the bed for leverage and tried again. She yanked with all her strength. The boot came off so suddenly that she lost her footing and fell backward to the carpet on her butt. But she had the boot in her hand.

Never one to do things halfway, she got to her feet and grabbed the other boot. This time she was prepared and maintained her balance. She placed both boots by the bed. She made to leave but thought he looked so uncomfortable. Grabbing a pillow, she stuffed it beneath his head. That was better.

Her hand went to undo the buttons on his shirt, but as soon as her fingers touched his masculine skin she drew back. She wouldn't go that far. He wouldn't appreciate it. Giving him one last look, she walked to the den.

She didn't feel right leaving and she still needed to talk to him. Without a second thought, she marched back to the bedroom and grabbed the other pillow. She'd sleep on the sofa. In the morning they'd discuss the DNA test.

BRODIE WOKE UP to thunder and realized it was inside his head. Oh, man. He clutched his head with both hands. What the hell? Patches of foggy memory began to drift across his aching brain.

After talking to his mother, he'd stopped in at the Boots and Spurs. He had a beer, then another and another. He'd had some whiskey in there, too. The more he drank, the better he felt.

He sat up and saw that he was hanging off part of the bed. At least he'd made it home and managed to remove his boots. He needed coffee, lots of coffee. As he stood, the room swayed and he sat back down. What a mess. He hadn't been that drunk in a long time.

Before he stopped at the bar, he drove around unable to get the DNA test out of his mind. All of his life he'd known exactly who he was—Thomas and Claudia Hayes's son, their cowboy disappointment. Now he wasn't so sure. Doubts mingled with fact and fiction. Who was he?

Light-headed, he made his way down the hall. His

one goal was to make a pot of strong coffee, but then he realized he had to use the bathroom. A quick stop and he proceeded to the den. He stopped short at the sight on his couch.

A woman lay on her stomach, her blond hair splayed across a pillow. Jeans molded her perfect bottom and sneakers lay tumbled on the floor. She was sound asleep.

Alex Donovan.

He vaguely remembered her at the bar. Bits and pieces filtered through the fog. She'd taken his keys so she must have driven him home. Where in the hell was his truck?

He walked to the window and saw her Jeep parked at the back door. That meant his truck was still at the bar. Damn. He had to go get it. The pounding in his head reminded him he had another emergency. Coffee.

Quickly making a pot, he glanced at the sleeping Alex. Besides Helen Braxton, she was the last person he wanted to see.

Chapter Seven

The smell of coffee woke Alex. She stretched and sat up, yawning, but clamped her mouth shut when she saw Brodie sitting in a chair, coffee cup in hand, watching her.

"Where's my truck?"

His neatly combed hair was still damp from a shower he'd obviously just taken. He'd shaved and changed his clothes and his boots were back on his feet. Pushing back her hair with both hands, she ignored that flutter in her stomach.

"Good morning to you, too."

"Where's my truck?" The dimple was nowhere in sight.

"At the bar."

He took a swallow of coffee. "If anything happens to that truck, I'm holding you responsible."

She lifted an eyebrow. "Do you not realize how drunk you were last night?"

He stared into his cup.

"Even the bartender knew you'd reached your limit. He refused to serve you any more beer. I'm sorry, but I wasn't letting you drive in that condition."

"My friends would have seen me home and taken care of my truck."

"I didn't see any friends around."

"Maybe because you were with me. They're not going to interfere while I'm with a woman."

"Well, pardon me for trying to help. And let me tell you it wasn't easy maneuvering your big frame into the house. Drunk, you weigh a ton. Nor was it a piece of cake getting your boots off."

His eyes narrowed. "You took off my boots?"

"Yes. Is that a crime, too?"

"Thanks," he mumbled as he took a sip from his cup. Some of his tension seemed to ebb away.

"If you don't mind, I'd like a cup of coffee."

"Suit yourself."

She found a cup in the cabinet and poured coffee into it. He didn't seem inclined to offer any assistance so she searched until she found sugar and milk. Taking a few sips, she went back to the den. She curled her feet beneath her and continued to drink her coffee.

"What were you doing at the bar?" he asked.

"I wanted to let you know that I was informing Mrs. Braxton of the DNA results."

"How did you know where to find me?"

"P.I.'s instinct."

"Or you got lucky."

"Maybe." She took a sip and the silence became unbearable. Biting her lip she ventured into treacherous territory. "The result was the same as the first test."

"Yep. Bet you're happy about that."

"Not exactly."

He frowned. "Then why are you doing this?"

"I'm a P.I. and it's my job. Mrs. Braxton had a folder of information about you, including photos. She knew your name and that you lived on a ranch outside Mesquite. She just wanted to know if you were the baby that was stolen from the nursery forty years ago. Mothers are funny like that. They never let go of a child even when it's taken from them."

She expected another sharp retort, but he set his cup on the end table and ran the palms of his hands up his face and through his hair. "I don't understand how I could be her son." His words were full of anguish and she felt a tug at her heart.

"Did you speak to your mother?"

"Yes. She says it's ridiculous. She wasn't even angry because it's so absurd."

Alex moved uneasily. "But you know something's wrong?"

"Yeah." He raised his eyes to hers. "You're the investigator. How could this happen?"

She placed her cup on the coffee table. "The baby switch would be quite simple if you both were in the hospital at the same time, but your mother and you were checked out two days before Helen Braxton was admitted."

"So someone had to have gone into the hospital and stolen Travis Braxton?"

"Yes."

"So where is Brodie Hayes?"

"That's a mystery. I checked records back then and there were no baby deaths reported during that period."

"So my mother is lying or something else is going on."

"Yes. Either way, there's a baby missing."

The silence returned in full force as he stared at the case of his rodeo memorabilia. Inside there was a photo of three cowboys, their arms around each other. Brodie was in the center, the cowboy on the right had brown hair and the one on the left was blond—all tall, boldly handsome cowboys.

"Are those your friends?" she asked as he kept staring at the photo.

"They're my family," was his response.

"Your family?"

"I tried to do what my parents wanted, but a year of college was all I could take. It just wasn't for me. When I told my dad, he said if I gave up college I wasn't his son." He looked at her. "Guess he was right, huh?"

She inclined her head, not knowing how to answer that question. She knew that he didn't expect one. He was just trying to get through all the feelings that had shaped his life—all the feelings that had been fueled by a lie.

"So the cowboys in the photo became your family?"

"Yeah. Colter Kincaid is the one on the right. His father was a rodeo rider so he continued the family tradition. Tully, his father's friend, helped him. Tripp Daniels is on the left and he was estranged from his family as well, so we all had a common connection. They called us the three amigos."

"Do you still see them?"

"Sure. Colter lives not far from me and married the love of his life, Marisa. They have two children. Tripp reconciled with his family and moved to Bramble,

Texas. He's been married about eighteen months to a woman who captured his heart the first moment he met her. They have a six-month-old son and Jilly."

"Jilly?"

"She's Camila's daughter by Tripp's brother, Patrick. He was killed in a car accident before they could get married. It's a long and involved story, but after many years Tripp returned home because his family needed him. He and Camila found each other and they're very happy. Both my friends are happy, but…" His voice trailed away.

"But you don't think that kind of happiness is for you?" She finished his sentence.

He rubbed his hands together. "Nope, especially not now. My life has suddenly been ripped to hell."

She swallowed. "Have you talked to your friends?"

"Colter's in New York. Marisa's mother is from there and they go there every now and then with her parents. They should be home soon. I called Tripp, but they were having a family birthday party for Mrs. Daniels so I told him I'd call later. I had intended to make the party. With everything that's happening, I forgot about it."

"Maybe you can call him today."

His eyes caught hers. "Why? Do you think I need to talk to someone?"

"Frankly, yes." She didn't lie.

"I'm talking to you. Doesn't that count?" His eyes demanded an honest answer.

"Of course. I just feel bad being caught in the middle."

"Mmm." He looked down at his clasped hands. "Thanks for bringing me home last night."

"You're welcome."

The silence returned and Alex took a breath.

"Would you like to know something about the Braxton family?"

He stood in a jerky movement. "No. Don't do that. I don't want to know anything about them."

"It would be easier…"

A tap at the door stopped her. "Brodie, are you home?" a male voice shouted.

"I'm in the den," Brodie shouted back.

A tall cowboy walked in. Blond hair curled into his shirt collar—this had to be Tripp Daniels. He was older than the man in the photo, but Alex knew it was him.

"Tripp, what are you doing here?" Brodie asked. They shook hands, then hugged briefly.

"I told Camila that you didn't sound right on the phone last night. After the party, I kept tossing and turning and Camila finally said to go see what was wrong. I headed out early this morning. I know you wouldn't have missed the party if…" He stopped as he saw Alex sitting on the sofa. "Oh, man. I'm sorry to intrude."

Before Alex could speak, Brodie said, "It's not what you think. This is Alex Donovan. She's a private investigator."

Tripp frowned, clearly not understanding anything.

Feeling out of place, she gathered her hair together and searched on the sofa for her clip. Running her hand between the cushions, she finally located it and clipped back her hair. It gave her some semblance of order, even though her emotions were disorganized and muddled.

"What's going on?" Tripp asked.

"Have a seat," Brodie replied, and Tripp took the chair Brodie had vacated. Brodie sat on the sofa next to her. "Remember all those times I told you I had to be adopted?"

"Yes."

"Well, it's worse than that. Alex was hired by Helen Braxton to find her son—a son who was stolen from the nursery almost forty years ago."

"Are you saying…"

"Yep. I'm Helen Braxton's biological son."

Tripp pulled off his hat and scratched his head. "Have you talked to your mother?"

"She said it's ridiculous and a lie. Aunt Cleo was there when I was born and she stayed with my mother until they brought me home." He stood abruptly. "I don't know what the hell's going on. Last night I got so drunk that Alex had to drive me home."

"I wondered where your truck was."

"If you have time, could you take me to the Boots and Spurs?"

The phone rang, preventing Tripp from responding. Brodie went into the kitchen to answer it.

"I'm glad you're here," Alex said to Tripp. "He's going to need someone to talk to."

"We're there for each other, no matter what," Tripp replied, and paused. "Is this for real?"

"Yes."

Brodie came back, his sun-browned skin a pasty yellow.

"What is it?" Alex was immediately on her feet.

"My mother…had…a massive heart attack."

Alex grabbed her shoes. "I'll get you to the hospital in no time. Let's go. I know all the shortcuts."

"I'll follow," Tripp called as they went out the door.

Alex didn't have time to put on her sneakers. She jumped into the driver's seat and started the engine. Brodie crawled in and sat as if turned to stone.

"She'll be fine," Alex said.

"I don't think so. Her heart was weak already. I should never have told her."

"You can't blame yourself." She whizzed onto the freeway.

"Who do I blame, Alex?" She felt the heat of his eyes on her. "Tell me. Who do I blame?"

She took an exit without slowing down and drove through a yellow light. "You can blame me. I took the case."

"That would be too easy." He shifted nervously in his seat. "Does this thing go any faster?"

"I'm breaking the speed limit now." She whipped down a side street and the hospital came into view. Pulling into the circular drive, she braked to a stop.

Brodie jumped out. "Thanks."

It took Alex ten minutes to find a parking place and thirty seconds to get her shoes on, then she hurried inside.

At the information desk she was told that Mrs. Hayes was in CCU and not allowed visitors. Only immediate family was allowed in at the appropriate times. She thanked the lady and walked off. Having visited this hospital before, she knew where the CCU unit was located.

She took the elevator to the fourth floor. There was a waiting room with phones and vending machines. It was full and she didn't see Brodie anywhere. Turning down a hall, she saw him talking to a lady with graying brown hair. She started to turn and leave, but she had to know how Mrs. Hayes was doing. Taking a seat down the hall, she waited.

"How IS SHE?" Brodie asked Cleo.

"The doctor hasn't told me anything, but I couldn't deal with this alone so I called you."

Brodie was taken aback. "What are you talking about? When did mother have the heart attack?"

"About two this morning."

"What! And you're just now calling me?"

"She wouldn't let me. Before she went out the last thing she said was not to call you."

"Cleo, that doesn't make any sense. Why would she not want you to call me? And why would you listen to her?"

"Claudie was acting very strange last night. She woke up screaming and when I went into her room she said she'd had a bad dream. Then I heard her gasping for breath. I immediately called 9-1-1 and when I tried to call you she became more agitated."

"Cleo…"

Dr. Finley, Claudia's cardiologist, came out of CCU and Brodie rushed to his side. "How's my mother?"

"Follow me," Dr. Finley said and walked into a small room. He turned to face Brodie. "I'm not going to lie to you. Your mother's had a massive heart attack and I'm not sure why she's still alive. Her heart has weakened considerably. She came around about an hour ago and she's in an agitated state. She's not making a lot of sense, so be prepared when you see her. We're trying to keep her calm. Seeing you might help."

Brodie swallowed. "How long does she have?"

"I don't know. We're monitoring her and doing everything we can. Surgery is out of the question. She wouldn't survive it."

"When can I see her?"

"I'll take you to her, but like I said, be prepared."

Brodie had had to face a lot of things in his life and he wondered if he was ready for this. He followed Dr. Finley into the unit. Beds were partitioned off with curtains. The nurse's station was in the center of the room so they could see and monitor each patient.

He stopped short when the doctor pulled back the curtain. His mother lay there, lifeless and pale. A monitor was attached to her heart and she was getting oxygen. His knees suddenly felt weak.

"Claudia, your son is here," Dr. Finley said.

His mother moaned and moved her head. Against the white sheets her skin looked almost gray.

"Can you hear me?" Dr. Finley asked.

"Bro-die," she moaned.

"He's right here." The doctor motioned for Brodie to come to the bed.

His boots felt like lead as he moved to her bedside. "Mother."

Claudia groped for his hand and he took it, thinking how fragile her fingers were.

"I'll give you a few minutes," the doctor said.

"Bro-die."

"It's okay, Mother. You don't have to talk."

"Have to, please."

"Okay, but don't get upset." There was a straight back chair in the small cubicle and Brodie used his free hand and pulled it forward. He held her hand in both of his.

"You were the…light in your father's eyes."

"I know."

"I…I…never saw him so happy as when he held you…for the first time. He had so many dreams for you."

He swallowed hard. "I'm sorry I let him down."

"You…never let us down." She squeezed his hand. "We let you down. I…I let you down."

"Mother…"

"When you asked about Helen Braxton, I didn't recognize the name because…I'd wiped it from my mind. Last…last night it all came back."

"You knew Helen Braxton?" His throat felt like gritty sand.

"No. I've never met her." Claudia took several breaths. "But years ago Cleo mailed the announcement of your birth in the Dallas paper and…I read where her son had been stolen."

He licked his dry lips. "Do you know how that happened?"

"Yes." She gulped for air. "I took him."

Chapter Eight

He swallowed twice before he could find his voice. "You took him!"

"Yes. Last night I remembered every horrible detail."

"What happened?" His voice was low and hoarse and he tried to maintain control of the emotions he was feeling at her admission.

"My baby was so beautiful. His black hair and blue eyes were just like Tom's. I couldn't wait for him to see his son." As she talked Brodie noticed her voice became stronger. "The doctor said it was okay to fly when you were a week old. You were very healthy so we had no problems. The night before we were to leave Harold called wanting to talk to Cleo. I told her to go ahead, I probably wouldn't sleep anyway. I was too excited about seeing Tom."

She stopped and Brodie asked, "What happened next?"

"I fell asleep. When I awoke about three, I realized my baby hadn't stirred and fussed for his feeding like he usually did. I crawled out of bed to feed him and he was lying so still, so lifeless. As I picked him up I realized he wasn't breathing. I shook and shook him…when I knew he was dead I went a little insane. I tried calling Cleo, but I couldn't reach her. I don't know why I didn't call for help. All I knew was that our son had died while I slept and I could never tell Tom that. He'd never forgive me."

She took a breath. "Somewhere in the insanity of my mind I reasoned that my son was still at the hospital. This dead child wasn't mine. I got dressed and found Cleo's car keys. Harold had come by the house to get her, so her car was in the garage. When I reached the hospital, I went inside and up to the nursery. The place was in semidarkness…no one was in the halls. Two nurses were on duty. I waited until they both answered calls then I slipped inside to the babies. There were seven of them and I looked at each one, searching for my son. Then I saw your black hair and I picked you up. You stretched and opened your eyes. They were blue and I knew I'd found my baby. I grabbed a sheet and wrapped you in a bundle and quickly left the hospital. No one saw me."

Brodie's chest felt tight and he struggled to breathe. "What did you do with your baby?"

Claudia flinched. "Cleo was working on her yard and earlier in the week she'd laid some paving stones to a gazebo she had in the back. I put my baby in a box, got a shovel from the garage and went outside. I pried up one of the stones, then dug a deep hole. I buried my baby and positioned the stone back in place. When morning came I cleaned up the excess dirt. Nothing looked out of place. I called for a cab and went to the airport. I slept for a long time on the flight. When I woke up, I didn't remember the night before. I felt drugged, but I had my son and soon we'd see Tom."

She paused. "I remembered it for the first time in a dream last night. It wasn't a dream, though. It actually happened."

"So I'm not your son?" After all she'd told him, he needed to hear her say it.

She groped for his hands. "No. You're not my son. But I loved you with all my heart. Your father did, too."

"Why are you telling me now?"

"So you'll know the truth from me, even though the DNA has already told you. I know I don't have much time left and I have to beg for your forgiveness. Please don't hate me."

Suddenly Brodie had reached his breaking point. He shoved back his chair. "I need some time." Before he could stop himself, he ran from the room.

ALEX SAW Brodie head for the exit and she jumped up to follow him. Down three flights of stairs she trailed him, taking the steps three at a time. When she reached the bottom floor, she didn't see him among the crowd of people. She quickly checked other exits, then she spotted him on a garden patio for visitors. Opening the door, she stepped out into the warm summer day. Because of the heat, they were the only two people on the patio.

He bent over, his hands on his knees, gulping in air. She gave him time.

He straightened and saw her. "Go away."

"How is your mother?"

"Don't pretend you care."

She ignored that tone in his voice, knowing he was hurting. "I do care. I started this, so I feel responsible."

Sinking onto a bench, he buried his face in his hands. "I can't believe this. I just can't."

She sat by him. "I know it's hard, but—"

"You don't understand."

"Then enlighten me."

He raised his head and looked at her, his eyes a stormy blue. "My mother told me the truth."

"Oh." She was taken aback for a moment. "What happened?"

He looked down at the concrete and told her all the details. "She wanted me to forgive her and I couldn't."

"That's probably a normal reaction."

He dragged his hands through his hair. "I'm not Brodie Hayes and I'm not Travis Braxton. Who the hell am I?"

Unable to resist, she reached out and hugged him. He gripped her so tight she thought her ribs might snap. But she didn't mind. At least he wasn't pushing her away. The heat from the concrete enveloped them and his aftershave and musky male scent filled her senses. Even with the heat, she thought she could hold him for the rest of her life.

The thought steadied her more than shocked her. She'd never felt about anyone this way and she didn't have time to figure out why.

She drew back slightly. "You know in your heart who you are, and in the days ahead that will become clearer."

"Maybe," he muttered.

"Would you like to hear about your biological family?"

"No," he snapped. "Please stop asking me that."

"I have to tell Mrs. Braxton."

"Then do, but don't expect anything from me."

"Okay." She stood and held out her hand.

He stared at her with a blank expression.

"Let's go see how your mother is. In your heart, she's still your mother."

Without a protest, he placed his hand in hers and they went back into the hospital.

ON THE FOURTH FLOOR, Tripp came toward them. "Where have y'all been? I've been looking everywhere."

"I'll let you talk to your friend," Alex said. "I'll be back later."

"Thanks, Alex," Brodie said, his eyes holding hers.

She nodded and walked toward the elevators.

Brodie watched until the doors closed.

"Is there something going on with you and the P.I.?" Tripp asked.

"I don't think so," he replied. "But then, I'm not too sure of anything at the moment."

"That's an odd answer even for you."

"Wait till you hear the rest." They found chairs and Brodie told his friend what his mother had told him.

"Damn. That's unbelievable." Tripp twirled his hat in his hand.

"Try being the cowboy on the end that fall."

"I'm sorry, Brodie. I really am. What can I do?"

"Go home to your family."

"I'm not leaving you like this."

"We're not young, immature cowboys anymore. I have to handle this in my own way."

"Brodie…"

"Remember the vow?" Years ago, estranged from their families, they'd made a pledge to each other.

"*Amigos* forever or until that perfect woman comes along," Tripp said.

"You've found your perfect woman so go home to her. I'll call you if there's any change in my mother's condition."

Tripp stood. "I'll go home, but I'll be back tomorrow." Tripp didn't move, though. "Are you okay?"

Brodie looked up at his friend. "I've taken a hard knock, but you know me better than anyone. I've had them before and I've survived. I'll survive this."

"But you don't have to do it alone."

"This time I have to."

Tripp knew what he meant and they embraced before Tripp walked away.

Brodie tried to get his emotions under control, but all he could feel at that moment was the softness and gentleness of Alex.

In your heart, she's still your mother.

Alex was right. Claudia was his mother. He couldn't wipe away those feelings, not even with the sense of indignation, betrayal and deception inside him. *He wasn't Brodie Hayes.* He couldn't seem to get beyond that or its implications.

Alex said he knew who he was. Right now, he didn't. That would take time. Maybe forgiveness would, too.

ALEX MADE the phone call and headed for her office to meet with Helen and Maggie. As she walked in, Buck shouted at her, "Where the hell have you been?"

She turned to him with a lifted eyebrow. "You keeping tabs on me now?"

"You ran out of the house like a bat out of hell and you didn't come home all night."

"That never bothered you before."

"Well, Naddy was home before and she always knew where you were."

"But you'd never ask."

Buck threw up his hands. "Okay. You're fine, so I'm getting back to work."

"Good idea. I've got a meeting with a client in a few minutes."

Buck stopped in the doorway. "The Braxton case?"

"Yes."

"That's good. The woman needs to know."

"Yes. But this is not easy on Brodie Hayes."

She expected a reprimand about being too soft, but he shrugged and went back to his office, which wasn't like him at all. And he never questioned her whereabouts in her off time. Was that because he knew Naddy kept tabs on her? Hmm. She was learning more about her father. Maybe he cared about her in his own way.

She couldn't even imagine what Brodie was going through—to learn that his parents were really not his parents. Claudia Hayes, distraught over her son's death, had just walked into the hospital and taken Travis Braxton because he looked like her son. No one knew. No one suspected. By the time the investigation got under way Travis Braxton was in Germany and the Braxton family would never see him again.

Until now.

She heard the door open and Helen and Maggie walked in. A tall gray-haired man wearing jeans, boots and holding a hat in his hand, was with them. He had to be in his mid-sixties, fit and strikingly handsome. The lines around his eyes and mouth told another story, one of pain and suffering. His blank eyes completed a picture of a disheartened man. This had to be George Braxton, Brodie's biological father.

For a moment she just stared. Brodie favored him so much. No wonder Helen was so adamant about the cowboy in the photo being her son.

The introductions were made and the Braxtons took their seats. "I finally told George what I'd done," Helen said. "In forty-one years of marriage I've never been able to keep anything from him."

She reached for her husband's hand and he gave a fake smile. Alex saw the dimple in his cheek and it was as if a lightning bolt had struck her. These were Brodie's parents.

"Honey, why do you keep doing this? Our boy is gone, just like the others."

This was going to be a wonderful moment for the Braxtons, except Brodie wasn't ready to accept them. She had to handle this very carefully.

"Is that true, Alex?" Helen asked. "Is Brodie Hayes not our son?"

"Be patient, Mom," Maggie suggested, and Alex

could hear the nervousness in her voice. She'd probably been through this many times.

Alex opened the file and pulled the DNA test forward. "I'm not sure how to tell you this."

"Just spit it out," George said. "My wife refuses to accept reality."

Alex took a moment, then said the words out loud. "Brodie Hayes *is* your biological son."

No one moved or said a word. "What?" Helen asked, stunned.

"Brodie is your son, the baby who was stolen from the hospital."

"Ohmygod! Ohmygod!" Helen choked out.

"Is that true?" George asked, the color draining from his face.

Tears streamed down Helen's face, and Maggie went to her. The three of them stood holding on, hugging tight. "We found our boy," George muttered, wiping at his eyes.

Alex felt a catch in her throat and waited to tell them the rest of the story.

Maggie grabbed some tissues out of her purse for her parents. "Thank you, Alex. Thank you."

"I didn't do anything but get Brodie to agree to a DNA test. Your mother already suspected who he was."

"When can we see him?" Helen asked, taking her seat and dabbing at her eyes.

"We need to talk."

"Oh." Helen became very still. "Is there a problem?"

"Brodie's not taking this well. He needs time."

"I want to see my son," George demanded.

"It's not up to you or me, Mr. Braxton. It's up to

Brodie. He's not exactly a minor, so you'll have to wait until he's ready."

"Why doesn't he want to see us?" Helen asked, her voice full of hurt.

"His mother has had a heart attack and she's not expected to live. He's not going to do anything until he's resolved things with her."

"Is she the one who stole him from the hospital?" George asked.

"Yes." Alex folded her hands in her lap and told them the whole story.

"She has no rights," George shouted. "She's a kidnapper." The despondent man who'd walked into her office was fast disappearing.

She took a deep breath. "It's not about rights. It's about Brodie's life. Mrs. Hayes is in no condition to offer any resistance. She's the one who told Brodie the truth about his birth and he's still at the hospital. That should tell you something. If you pressure him or push him in any way, you'll lose him for good this time. I'm certain about that."

"I don't understand." George shook his head. "I just want my son back—my oldest son."

Maggie rubbed his shoulder. "Dad, don't get upset. We found Travis. That's good news."

"What good is it if he doesn't want anything to do with us?"

Alex wished she could explain this to their satisfaction, so she tried again. "That baby who was stolen is gone forever. There's a man in his place now. A man who has had parents all his life—parents he's loved. It's not easy to make that one-hundred-and-eighty-degree turn to another set of parents. He's going through a great deal and as his biological parents you should be willing to give him time to adjust. Time that he needs."

"Is his father living?" George asked.

"No. He died several years ago."

"So he has just the woman in the hospital?" Helen asked, and Alex noticed she didn't say mother.

"Yes, and an aunt."

"I can't believe she took our son." Helen blinked, as if she couldn't grasp all the details, then moaned a pitiful sound. "All the time the police were looking for our baby he was in Germany."

"Yes. Brodie was two years old when they came back to the States."

"All those years I wondered. All those years —now I know."

"Yes, Helen. That's the good news. Your son is alive and well. Now he needs your patience and understanding. Give him a week and I'll speak with him again. Right now he's in a state of denial, but eventually he will want to meet you."

"Then I guess we'll wait."

"I don't like it," George said, getting to his feet.

Helen picked up her purse. "Tell him we love him. We're his parents."

Alex stood also. "That's the problem. He hasn't made the transition yet."

"I'm trying to understand."

"Thanks, Helen. Down the road I feel there will be a happy ending."

Helen dug in her purse and pulled out a silver baby rattle wrapped in blue velvet. "I've held onto this memento. Sometimes I didn't understand why. Now I do. As long as I had it I knew there was hope that one day I would see him again. Please give it to him." She handed the rattle to Alex. On it was inscribed *George Travis Braxton Jr.* and the date he was born.

A lump formed in Alex's throat. "I will."

"Thank you, Alex, and please stay in touch."

The threesome left the office and she stared down at the rattle. It was shining just as bright as the future that Travis Braxton should've had. Somehow Alex knew that he still could have it and she had to make it happen. Though her heart was clearly on Brodie's side, there had to be a way for the Braxton family to come together again.

Chapter Nine

Alex finished some paperwork and went into Buck's office. "I'm taking the next couple of days off."

He leaned back in his chair. "Really?"

"Yes." She looked him squarely in the eye. "There's nothing that's pressing right now and I need this time."

Buck folded his hands behind his head. "Where you going?"

"It's personal."

"Mmm." He leaned forward. "Brodie Hayes."

"Maybe. Maybe not. It's my business."

"Girl…"

"See you later." She hurried for the door. That might be the coward in her, but she didn't want to hear his take on Brodie.

She sat in her Jeep, wondering what to do about Brodie's truck. Her cell buzzed and she clicked on. It was Tripp Daniels.

"I'm at Brodie's and I can't find his truck keys," Tripp said. "Your number is scribbled on a pad so I thought I'd check with you since you brought him home. I want to get his truck home."

"I have them. The truck is at the Boots and Spurs. I'll meet you there."

They debated where to take the truck and ended up driving it to the Cowboy Up Ranch. If something happened to Mrs. Hayes, they figured Brodie wouldn't be in any shape to drive.

She picked up Tripp and drove him to his truck. He talked about his wife and kids, his family and Brodie. It was clear he was a happily married man.

"I'm going home, but I'll be back tomorrow," Tripp told her.

"Brodie's going to need his friends."

"We'll be there." He crawled out of her Jeep. "Nice talking to you."

These cowboys stuck together. She admired that.

SHE WENT HOME, turned on the sprinklers, then hurried inside and showered. Curling up on her bed, she called Naddy.

"Hey, honeychild, how you doing?"

"That's what I'm wondering about you," Alex replied.

"I've having the time of my life. Ethel and me are going to a strip show tonight. I plan to tuck a lot of dollar bills in a G-string."

"Naddy, for heaven sakes, strippers are very young men."

"So? I might be old, but I'm not dead."

Alex sighed. "When are you coming home?"

"In a couple of days, but if I win at slots again Ethel and me might stay a while."

"Naddy…"

"Don't bitch, Alex. You sound like Buck."

"I just worry about you."

"I know, honeychild."

"And I miss you." She wanted her grandmother to come home. She needed to talk to her. With her girlfriends married and living away, she felt so alone at times. She sat up. What was wrong with her? She had witnessed so much heartache today and she needed to hug someone. Soon she'd have to get that life she was always telling herself about. Hell, her grandmother had more fun than she did.

"You have a great time," Alex added.

"I always do," Naddy replied. "And I got those cops to listen to me about the missing girl. They're checking it out."

"That's good. I'll see you in a couple of days."

"You betcha."

Alex hung up the phone and stared at it for a moment, then she jumped up and dressed. She grabbed a Popsicle before going out the door. Turning off the sprinklers, she headed for the hospital.

Eating a Popsicle and driving was probably something she shouldn't be doing, but she managed. She found a parking spot and applied lipstick and realized her tongue was red. Damn. Well, who was going to look at her tongue?

She took the elevator to the CCU unit, but she didn't see Brodie. So she found a seat, picked up a magazine and waited.

BRODIE AND Cleo walked out of the unit.

"At least she's sleeping now," Cleo said.

"Yeah."

"I'm sorry, Brodie. I had no idea she'd done such a thing."

"Thanks, Cleo. It's just a little hard to deal with."

"I can imagine. Just don't let it get you down, cowboy."

He tried to smile. "I may not know who I am, but I'm a cowboy. I've always known that."

"And you're a wonderful, compassionate, strong and hard-working man. You're smart, honest, loyal and—"

"Whoa. Don't get carried away."

"I love you, Brodie. You're like my own son." She hugged him and he hugged her back. *She's not my aunt,* he thought. But his heart didn't know that.

Cleo drew back. "Claudie seems at peace."

"I think the truth has given her some kind of atonement."

"Forgive her, Brodie. For yourself, forgive her."

He looked into his aunt's eyes. "I wish it was that simple."

Cleo touched his arm. "Think I'll go home and get a few hours sleep."

"That's a good idea."

"See you in the morning."

Brodie walked down the hall to a water fountain, just to do something. He stopped when he saw Alex sitting in the waiting room. How long had she been here?

She looked up and immediately came to his side.

"What are you doing here?" he asked.

"I wanted to check on your mother and see how you were doing."

"My mother's holding her own. I'm in a fog. I'm not really sure what I'm doing."

"I'm so sorry."

"I wish people would stop saying that." He sucked in a quick breath. "You can leave now. I can handle this, I don't need a babysitter."

"I know you don't."

"Oh, man." He paused as something hit him. "You're here about the Braxtons, aren't you?"

"Not really. But I did tell them."

He held up a hand. "I don't want to hear it."

"Fine. I won't until you're ready."

His eyes held hers. "I may never be ready." The thought of the Braxtons expecting him to be their son was making him ill. How could he explain that to Alex without hurting her. "I have to get back to my mother."

He walked to Claudia's bedside and tried to stop thoughts of Alex. She was just another complication he didn't need right now.

"Brodie?"

"Yes, Mother. It's me." He took a seat by her bed. The doctor had arranged for him to come and go as he pleased and he was glad about that. If he left, he'd probably never return. That was a hard truth. He knew there were a lot more to come.

"Where's Cleo?"

"She went home for a while."

"Good, and you need to get some rest, too."

"I can't sleep."

"I'm so sorry, son."

He shifted uneasily at that word. "You keep saying that, but it doesn't change anything. For years I've had so many guilty feelings for disappointing you and Dad. Now everything has changed and I'm not sure what to feel. I'm numb inside."

"Brodie, you're strong and you will recover from this. You will be stronger."

"At what price?"

A moan left her throat. "Don't hate me. Please don't hate me."

All his life he had a problem talking to his mother. He'd rather have a root canal, but here he sat pouring out his feelings in a way that surprised him.

"If I hated you, I wouldn't be here."

"Thank you."

Suddenly memories of his childhood flashed through his mind. "Remember when I was six or seven and you bought that sailor outfit for me?"

"Yes. You ripped it off and refused to wear it. You only wanted to wear jeans and sneakers. That is, until you discovered cowboy boots."

"Dad threw out my first pair."

"You bought them with your allowance at a thrift shop when you were out with a friend. We weren't letting you put your feet in them. We didn't know who had owned them."

"I was mad, though."

"You were mad a lot as a teenager."

"Yeah. That's why I had to leave. I guess I was

searching for the real me." As the words slipped out, he knew they were true.

"Please forgive me." Claudia fumbled for his hand.

Through the semidarkness he stared at her frail fingers. Those hands had made him peanut butter and jelly sandwiches, bandaged his scraped knees when he fell and they held his face every night and kissed his forehead before he went to sleep. *This was his mother. Had been for forty years.* Just like that he knew he could say what she needed to hear.

"I forgive you." He heard his words but he wasn't sure he meant them. He'd said them, though, that was the important part.

"Thank you," she whispered, and drifted into sleep.

He slowly made his way out of the room, feeling drained, but also experiencing a release that he couldn't explain.

WALKING INTO the waiting room, he stopped short. Alex sat there. It was almost midnight and no one else was in the room. Her sneakers lay on the floor, her knees were drawn up to her chin and her head rested on them. Several strands of hair had come loose from the clip and hung down her neck. This lady just never gave up. But he had to admit he was glad to see her.

He sat beside her and she raised her head to look at him. Her eyes were glazed with sleep and he thought she probably looked like that first thing in the morning. Even though he'd seen her this morning, he hadn't noticed because he was angry with her for interfering in his life.

"Why are you still here?" he asked.

She shrugged. "Guilt. Worry. Stupidity."

"Stupidity?"

"Yeah. When a man keeps telling me not to come back, you'd think that after a while I'd get the message."

"Mmm." He rested an ankle on his knee. "You must have a hard head."

"Not near as hard as my dad's."

He looked at Alex and realized he knew very little about her. "You said your dad's name is Buck?"

She curled her feet beneath her, getting comfortable. "Yes. The one and only Dirk Donovan, ex-cop and now a P.I. We're partners in Donovan Investigations. Or at least that's the way it's supposed to be, but Buck makes it very clear he's the boss."

"Are you an only child?"

"Yes. My mother died when I was two and my dad never remarried."

"So you're close?"

"Hardly." She gathered the stray strands and tugged them into the clip. "We don't see eye-to-eye on much of anything. I had a very unconventional childhood."

"In what way?"

"When my mother died, my grandmother moved in to help with me. Buck and Naddy get along like cats and dog. He snarls and she scratches back. My grandmother's not a conventional-type grandmother. She was a bail bondsman until she retired. After school, I did my homework in her office and I saw a lot of criminals. Naddy made me stay in the back room, but I always peeped out to see what was going on. I guess that's why I became a cop. It's in my genes."

He rubbed the leather on his boot. "So you were a cop?"

"Yes. For several years."

It was so easy to talk to her and that's what he needed. To talk about something that wouldn't drag him down. And he was intrigued by her.

"Is your grandmother still living?"

"Oh, yes. At the moment she's in Vegas gambling and trying to get the Vegas police's attention."

"Why?"

"Since she retired, she does a lot of searching on the Internet looking for missing children. She thinks she's found one and she's trying to get that across to the police."

"Sounds like a very interesting lady."

"That's my Naddy."

He studied the tip of his boot. "There's a lot of missing kids in this world."

"Sad, but yes."

"Too bad Naddy wasn't looking for me. Maybe I would've grown up a cowboy."

"But you are a cowboy," she reminded him.

He was—nothing in his childhood had changed that. "I guess that dominant gene prevailed."

"The Braxton—"

"Don't do that," he warned.

"Please don't keep pushing these people away. They're hurting and they need to see you."

He stood in one easy movement. "Is that why you're here—to keep pressuring me?"

"No. I'm here because of you." Her brown eyes didn't waver from his.

"Why? You don't even know me."

"Maybe not. But I can feel your pain." She pointed at him. "And don't laugh at that. I'm told my mother was the same way. That's why my father says I'll never make a great P.I. I let myself get too involved."

He frowned, hearing the pain in her voice. "Your father told you that?"

"I told you we don't have the best relationship."

He eased back into his chair. "Tom expected great things of me. He became a general like his father and he wanted the same of me. It took every ounce of courage I had to tell them how I felt. Tom said I'd become a loser and amount to nothing. To prove him wrong drove me every day of my life."

"Did you see your parents often after that?"

"No. I didn't see them for years. My father said you leave college, that's it. He was a very strict man. He meant it."

"When did you start seeing your parents again?"

"I called them one Christmas. My dad started coming to the rodeos soon after that. Not often, but every now and then. He was there when I won big in Vegas. All I could think that night was I couldn't lose with my dad watching me." He stopped for a moment as he remembered all the emotions, the energy that drove him. His dad was there and he had to make him proud because of the hurt he'd caused him. *But he wasn't my father.* The reality of that was almost too painful to bear.

"So you started seeing them?"

"What? Oh." He'd become completely lost in his

thoughts until he heard her soft voice. "Not really. My dad died a few months later and that's when my mom and I started seeing each other again. She moved to Dallas to be near Cleo, her sister...and later I settled in Mesquite." He leaned forward, his elbows on his knees. "I always had a problem talking to my parents. I'd get this huge knot in my stomach and I lived on Pepto-Bismol. But when I was talking to my mother tonight, I didn't get that knot. We talked like mother and son. She asked me to forgive her...and I said the words. I didn't think I'd be able to, but I did."

"Did you mean them?"

"I'm not sure. She was suffering and I wanted to stop that."

She touched his arm as if she understood.

He stared down at her fingers, soft as a baby's yet sensuous as a woman's. A sense of anticipation filled him, like a kid about to unwrap an unexpected gift. His mind was a mess and he decided he was delusional. Sex was the furthest thing from his mind. But she was one helluva woman.

He cleared his throat. "It was the only thing I could do."

"Brodie Hayes, you're going to be fine."

He looked into her sparkling eyes. "You think so?"

She tilted her head and smiled. "I've always heard cowboys are tough."

"Really? Uhh..." He was staring at her mouth.

"What?"

"Your tongue is red."

"Oh, no." She stood on her knees to look at herself in the glass pane.

"Take my word. It's red."

She sank back on her heels. "Damn. I was eating a Popsicle earlier. That food coloring must last forever."

"You like Popsicles?"

She made a face. "Yes. And don't tell a soul. Naddy swears I'm still six."

"You're anything but six." His eyes met hers and he felt the tension—that good, hot-and-bothered sexual tension. He wasn't delusional. He was thinking about her in ways that he shouldn't. But…

"Brodie." Dr. Finley stood in the doorway.

His thoughts came to a screeching halt. If the doctor was here this time of night, then something had to be wrong.

He was immediately on his feet. "What is it?"

"The nurse said you were down here so…"

"Is this about my mother?"

"Yes. Brodie, I'm sorry. We did everything we could, but she passed away a few minutes ago."

Chapter Ten

"I'm so sorry." The doctor patted Brodie on the shoulder, but he seemed to be in a trance.

"Would you like to see her?" Dr. Finley asked.

"No," Brodie answered. "I already said goodbye."

"Fine." The doctor patted his shoulder again and walked out.

Alex went to Brodie and wrapped her arms around him. "I'm sorry."

He held her in a fierce grip. His body trembled and her arms tightened around his waist. Time stood still for that brief moment. The smell of leather and antiseptic mingled around them. His stubble brushed her forehead and she breathed in the scent of his skin, which had a distinctive masculine appeal. It was a potent combination, but that wasn't what kept her holding on. He needed her—no one had ever needed her this much.

He suddenly drew back, his face solemn, pain etched in every feature. Claudia Hayes may not have been his biological mother, but that didn't make a difference now.

"I need to call Cleo, Colter and Tripp," he said, his voice hoarse. "And I have to make arrangements."

She caught his hand. "It's late. Sit for a while and talk to me."

He didn't offer any objection as he half fell into the chair. Leaning forward, he clasped his hands tightly. "This shouldn't be so hard. Why is it?"

"Because she was your mother and you loved her."

"She lied to me for so many years."

"You said she didn't remember stealing you from the nursery and I believe that. Don't you?"

He raised a clasped fist to his forehead and squeezed his eyes shut. "Yes." The word was barely audible.

Unable to stand that anguished look, Alex covered the fist with her hands. "It's okay to be sad. And it's okay to love the woman who raised you, even though you had a turbulent relationship. Biological kids have those, too."

The fist fell into his lap and he stared straight ahead. "All my life I felt like a square peg being forced into a round hole. Finally I couldn't take the pressure anymore." He took a deep breath. "I'm confused and numb right now."

She rubbed his arm, needing to touch him. "That's understandable."

He turned to look at her, his eyes wet. "Thank you for being here."

"You're welcome." His pain was almost more than she could take, but she had to keep him talking. He needed that more than anything.

"You said you told your mother you forgave her. Is that what you meant by saying goodbye?"

"Yes. I think we both knew it. Maybe that's why I was able to say the words."

"I'm glad you had the chance to talk to her without the anger."

"Me, too." He suddenly stood. "I better go. I have things to do."

"You don't have a vehicle," she reminded him.

"What? Oh yeah. My truck's still at the bar. Man, I've got to go." He whirled toward the door.

"Your truck's at home," she called to his retreating back.

He stopped in his tracks and glared at her. "Did you drive my truck?"

"Are you kidding?" She got to her feet. "Since you said I was responsible for it, I was worried how to get it back to your ranch. I didn't want anything to happen to that chunk of steel. Tripp saved the day. He drove it." Her eyes narrowed. "Is it okay for a cowboy to drive your truck?"

"Sorry. I'm on edge." His hand slipped through his hair, which was making it more disheveled. "I wonder where my hat is?"

"You didn't leave with it this morning."

"Oh. That's odd. I never go anywhere without my hat."

"You were rather upset."

"Mmm."

She reached for her purse. "Come on. I'll take you home."

Brodie spoke with the nurse then they made their way out of the hospital to her Jeep. He didn't say a word the whole drive back and Alex didn't push him.

It was after two when she parked at his house. Brodie held on to the dashboard with one hand.

"Did anyone ever tell you that you use this Jeep like a weapon?"

She turned off the lights and the interior flooded with darkness. Everything was so quiet, inside and outside. That peacefulness she'd experienced before settled over her.

"I refuse to answer on the grounds that it might incriminate me."

"I bet."

"The ride wasn't that bad." It was good to talk about something so inane.

"You went through three yellow lights. And, by the way, stop means stop, not breeze slowly through."

"Just be thankful I wasn't driving your truck."

"Women don't drive my truck."

"Are you serious?" She grinned at him in the darkness and could see he was absolutely serious. "You really have a fetish about that truck."

He opened his door and got out. "Remember that. And no wonder you couldn't get me in and out of this toy called a vehicle. It's like putting on a suit of armor."

She followed him to the door, knowing if he was griping he had to be feeling better. "It had nothing to do with the fact that you were drunk."

"A minor detail." He reached for his keys and realized he didn't have them.

She jangled them in front of him.

He took them without a word and opened the door.

But he didn't go in. "You can go home now. Your baby-sitting job is over."

She didn't move, wondering if she should leave him alone.

As if sensing her thoughts, he added, "I'm going to shower and change, then go see my aunt."

She still hesitated.

"I'll be fine, Alex. Thanks for everything you did today. I appreciate it."

"Good night, then." She turned and headed for her car. She couldn't treat him like a ten-year-old. He needed time alone.

"'Night. Drive carefully," he called after her.

"Ahh, don't know the meaning of the word."

She heard a sound and she wondered if it was a laugh or a curse. Either way she was smiling as she crawled into her vehicle. The smile didn't last. The day had been full of heartache and sadness. Driving away, she wondered how much more Brodie could take.

AT FIVE BRODIE was at his mother's home. So many times he'd made the trip with a knot in his gut. Maybe today it would be the last time. He had to tell Cleo.

They sat at the kitchen table, drinking coffee with Cleo crying sporadically. "All my life I tried to be there for Claudia, but when she needed me the most I wasn't there."

"You can't blame yourself for what happened."

"If I had been home instead of chasing after Harold, I would have been there for her."

Brodie toyed with his cup. "After that first DNA test, I kind of thought that you might have done something. I wasn't clear what, but I knew you'd do anything for Claudia."

Cleo eyes grew big. "Lordy, no. I'd never do such a thing."

"I can see that now."

Cleo sipped at her coffee. "Brodie?"

"Hmm?"

"What about the Braxton family?"

He stood and carried his cup to the sink. "I can't think about them right now." Rinsing his cup, he thought that someday soon he'd have to face the reality of the Braxton family. But not today.

He walked back to the table and they talked about Claudia and family, familiar things. "Why don't you get dressed so we can make arrangements."

"Your father is buried at Arlington National Cemetery and that's where Claudia wanted to be buried—with Tom."

"I'll get in touch with a military lawyer, but I thought it might be nice to have a service here for all her friends."

She touched his face with a trembling hand. "You're such a wonderful person."

"Thanks, Cleo. I don't feel too wonderful at the moment. I'm just trying to get through this."

"I know, sweetie. I'll throw some clothes on and we can go to the funeral home."

While he waited he called Tripp and Colter. Colter and his family had made it home from New York late last night and both Colter and Tripp wanted to come, but he assured them it wasn't necessary. He didn't tell Colter about his paternity. He had to do that face-to-face.

All the while Brodie was making arrangements he kept thinking that someone else needed a proper burial. Baby Brodie Hayes. And he knew someone who could help him. *Alex.*

ALEX HAD TAKEN time off because she'd thought that Brodie might need someone. She couldn't push herself on him, though, and he had his friends. Still, she'd check in with him today to make sure he was okay.

She had to call the Braxtons to let them know what had happened. They weren't going to be happy that Claudia's death would delay their meeting Brodie. Somehow Alex had to work this out.

She quickly showered, changed and headed downstairs. Buck was going to be surprised to see her. In the doorway to the kitchen she paused in complete shock. Buck and his lady friend, Connie, sat at the table eating breakfast. Buck never brought women to the house, but she guessed he thought she and Naddy were out so he didn't see a problem. And there wasn't one. Only in Buck's mind.

"Good morning, Buck, Connie," she said brightly.

Buck scrambled to his feet like a kid with his hand caught in the cookie jar. "Alex, I didn't know…you said…"

"You're stammering, Buck." Alex held out her hand to Connie. "I don't believe we've met, officially. I'm Alex, Buck's daughter."

"Nice to meet you." They shook hands. Connie was a medium-sized woman with short dyed red hair and a nervous smile.

"Connie stopped by for a cup of coffee," Buck said in a rush.

"In her bathrobe?" Alex lifted an eyebrow. "Give it up. I'm not six years old and there's no need to keep Connie a secret. I know she goes with you to the coast." She poured a cup of coffee.

"I thought you were taking some time off," Buck said, shifting gears.

"I was, but I've changed my mind." She opened the back door. "I don't mind if you have girls in your room, but, oh, wait till I tell Naddy."

"Alex…"

"Connie, stay as long as you like. As far as I'm concerned, you're welcome here any time."

"Alex…"

She smiled all the way to her car. Having the upper hand felt damn good. Again she thought she should have her own place. And Buck needed his privacy. But what about Naddy?

She couldn't think about that now. Other matters took precedence. She wondered how Brodie was this morning.

As soon as Alex reached the office, she called the Braxtons. Helen answered.

"Oh, Alex. I hope you have good news."

"Not really. Claudia Hayes passed away last night."

"Oh my goodness. How's Tra…I mean Brodie?"

"Not good. I just wanted to let you know that this is going to take longer than a week."

"Oh, dear. I'm trying to understand, but we're all so anxious. George is a completely different man. He looks forward to each day now. I don't know how to tell him this."

"Just be honest. That's all we can do now."

"I always thought if we ever found our son he would be as happy to see us as we are to see him."

"Just give it time," was all Alex could say.

She'd barely hung up when the phone rang. They had to hire a new receptionist, but Buck ran them off as fast as she could hire them. She might have to use a little blackmail with her father. The thought was tempting.

"Donovan Investigations," she said into the receiver.

"Alex Donovan, please," a male voice said.

"This is Alex."

"Ms. Donovan, this is Sergeant Talbot with the Vegas Police Department."

Alex sat up straight. Something had happened to Naddy. Her heart fell to the pit of her stomach.

"What's this about?"

"I have Nadene Donovan and Ethel Grimly in a cell and…"

Alex leapt to her feet. "What! Why do you have my grandmother locked up?"

"For disturbing the peace and being a public nuisance."

"What did she do?"

"They caused quite a ruckus at a strip club last night. Mrs. Donovan pulled the stripper's G-string down and all hell broke loose. Both women were more than a little intoxicated."

"Oh, my." Alex plopped into her chair.

"Listen, I'm not too thrilled about having women

that age in my jail. If you'll pay the fine and damages, I'll make sure they're on the next plane out of here."

"Yes. Thank you. Just tell me where to wire the money." She jotted down the information. "They have tickets so if you'll escort them to the airport, I'll meet them on this end."

"I'll see that it's done, and Ms. Donovan, don't send your grandmother to Vegas for a while."

"Don't worry. She won't be going anywhere for some time."

Alex hung up the phone fuming, then she started to pace. What was Naddy thinking? Naddy drank, but there were very few times Alex had seen her drunk. She must have really tied one on last night. Pulling down a stripper's G-string. Only Naddy would do something like that.

She paused as the humor of it hit her and she burst out laughing. It really wasn't a laughing matter, but she couldn't help it. Turning toward her chair, she froze. Brodie stood in the doorway.

"Morning." He removed his hat and walked in. "What's so funny?"

Her eyes soaked up his presence. He was clean-shaven and wearing starched clothes, looking so good he took her breath away. But she noticed the tired lines around his eyes and mouth. The bluest eyes in Texas were dull and the dimple wasn't in sight. It only made special appearances—happy appearances. Brodie's life hadn't been too happy lately.

"What's so funny?" he asked again.

"Nothing really. Just my grandmother." He

probably thought she was a lunatic or a woman who had mood swings.

"Didn't you say she was in Vegas?"

"Yeah." She told him about the call.

"Wow." He took a seat. "She *is* unconventional."

"And strange, arrogant and fearless."

"Do things like this happen often?"

"Too often."

"You must have had a fun childhood."

"Hardly. I wanted a grandmother who baked cookies, cleaned house and who had supper on the table at six with a big smile."

"The feminists would have a field day with that."

She shrugged. "What can I say? I watched too many reruns of *Leave It To Beaver* and *Andy Griffith*. Gotta love Aunt Bee."

They were making small talk as she waited for him to tell her why he was here.

He twisted his hat in his hand. "I made arrangements for my mother," he said. "We're having a service here, but she'll be buried at Arlington with my dad. My aunt and I are flying with the body."

"That's nice."

"I keep thinking about the baby that died."

"The real Brodie Hayes?"

He raised his eyes to look at her. "I want him to be buried with his mother."

Alex was taken aback for a moment. "You mean…"

"I'm not sure how to go about this and I thought you might know." He stood, reached in his pocket, pulled out a piece of paper and handed it to her. "That's the address where Cleo lived when Claudia's baby was born. Since you were a police officer, do you know how to go about handling this?"

She fingered the paper. "This is going to cause some publicity."

"I'd like to keep it as low-key as possible."

"I'll make some calls, but you do realize the Braxton family will be contacted."

He nodded. "That's okay as long as I don't have to see them."

"Brodie…"

"Sorry. At this time that's all I can do."

She wanted to say so many things, but words stuck in her throat. He had to make the transition on his own.

He stopped in the doorway. "My cell number and the address of the funeral home are on the back. If you'd like to come, the service is at ten, day after tomorrow."

"I'd like that."

His eyes held hers for a moment. "I would, too."

Chapter Eleven

Alex immediately went to work on retrieving Brodie Hayes's body. She knew people at the police station and they pointed her in the right direction. Detective Rod Stalwart had handled the Braxton baby's disappearance, but he'd retired years ago. Detective Mike Crane now had it in his cold case files.

She apprised Mike of the situation and she didn't get the usual runaround. In his late thirties, Mike was an eager beaver out to solve as many cold cases as he could. He was happy to have one laid in his lap.

Since time was of the essence, Mike began the paperwork for a court order. He said he'd be in touch.

Alex drove to the address Brodie had given her. The tan, frame house was in an older neighborhood and run down, the paint had peeled off in places and several screens were missing. Kids played in the front yard. On a hunch, she got out and walked over to them. Two girls giggled as they jumped rope on the sidewalk, reciting silly rhymes. A solemn-faced boy bounced a basketball against the house.

She approached the girls. "Is your mother home?"

The older one stopped jumping. "Yeah. What do you want?"

"I'd like to speak with her, please."

"Mama!" the girl screamed.

The door flew open and an overweight woman in skimpy shorts and a tank top stood there, puffing on a cigarette. "Rayann, how many times have I told you not to…" Her voice trailed off as she saw Alex.

"This lady wants to see you." Rayann thumbed toward Alex, and went back to jumping.

"Hi. I'm Alex Donovan, private investigator."

"Really?" The woman took a puff and blew out the smoke. "What are you doing here?"

Alex tried not to cough as the smoke filled up her nasal passages. "I'm working a case for a family who used to live in this house."

"Oh." Her eyes became enormous. "Was there a murder here or something?"

"May I come in?"

"Oh, sure. I'm Sueann Sims."

She followed Sueann into the cluttered living room and her eyes were drawn to the window with worn red drapes. With one hand she slightly edged back the drapes to see the backyard. No gazebo and no paving blocks. Damn. Her job got harder.

"You have a big backyard."

"That's why we bought the house, so the kids would have room to play." Sueann crushed her cigarette in an ashtray and moved laundry from the sofa. "Have a seat."

Alex kept standing. She didn't plan to be here that

long. "The lady who used to live here said there was a gazebo out back."

"Nope. Not when we moved here. The house was vacant for a long time and overgrown with weeds. We're just now getting it back into shape, or at least where we can mow it."

"The police will be contacting you today or tomorrow. We'll talk again then."

"I wish you'd tell me what this is about."

"The police will explain it." Alex walked to the door. "Thank you."

"Sure."

The girls were still jumping rope. "Gypsy, gypsy please tell me. What my future's going to be," the girls chorused.

Without thinking, Alex jumped into the rope with Rayann. "Rich man, poor man, beggar man, thief. Doctor, lawyer, Indian chief. Tinker, tailor, cowboy, sailor."

"You're good." Rayann grinned.

Alex laughed, jumped out and ran to her Jeep. That felt good and it released a lot of pent-up emotions. She and her friend Patsy spent years practicing a jumping routine. They thought they were cool. It seemed that little girls were still the same.

Inside the Jeep her heart raced. Was there a cowboy in her future? She reached for her cell phone and called Brodie to tell him about the gazebo.

"Damn. I guess it was too much to hope it would still be the same."

"Forty years is a long time."

"Is that a knock at my age?"

She smiled and closed her eyes, envisioning his dimple. "No. It's just fact."

"Mmm."

Alex thought it best to stay on business. "Could you get your aunt to draw a map of the backyard as she remembers it? It would make it easier for the detective."

"Sure. And thanks, Alex, for getting on this so fast."

"You're welcome, cowboy. Maybe one day you'll let me drive your big old truck."

"It only responds to me."

"Like your horse?"

"You bet."

"Cowboys have strange habits."

"Honey, if you only knew." She could feel a smile coming through the phone. And the way he said *honey* made her feel gooey and sweet inside.

"I'm going to click off on that one," she said. "Let me know when you get the map."

Her heart raced faster and she realized she was beginning to have strong feelings for Brodie. Just talking to him made her feel young and giddy. Looking at him, well, that sent her senses into a whirligig—big-time.

Was it sexual attraction? Or more?

LATE THAT AFTERNOON Mike informed her he had gotten the court order. She told him about the gazebo and that Brodie's aunt was drawing a map. They planned to start digging about ten the next morning. She was amazed at the speed in which Mike was able to get things done. But a forty-year-old cold case didn't get solved every day.

She called Brodie, but he didn't answer so she left

him a message. Then she headed for the airport to pick up Naddy and Ethel.

With the two offenders finally in the Jeep, she gave them a stern lecture.

"Alex, it was an accident," Naddy said. "I tucked a dollar in and my ring got caught. I jerked my hand and the damn string came down and his jewels spilled out, so to speak. And the women went crazy. But those were some mighty fine jewels. Don't you think so, Ethel?"

"Couldn't take my eyes off 'em."

"The damages were fifteen hundred dollars, not to mention the fine. This is not a freebie. It's coming out of your social security."

"Whatever. A woman can't even have fun anymore."

She gave Naddy a sideways glance. "When you damage other people's property, it's not fun. It's a crime."

"Those crazy women did that. Ethel and me were trying to get out of the way."

"You caused the scene." Alex was trying hard to be firm, but she was going to burst out laughing at any moment.

"We had a good time otherwise," Ethel said from the backseat.

Alex glanced in the rearview mirror at Ethel. "Good. Because I'm wondering how to punish two grandmas."

Naddy pinched her cheek. "With a smile."

They dropped Ethel at her daughter's and it took a few minutes to get her out of the backseat. Alex decided she definitely needed a different car. This vehicle was for a young girl and she had suddenly matured.

On the drive to the house, Naddy asked, "What did you tell Buck?"

"Nothing. I'll let you tell him."

Naddy pinched her cheek again. "You're a shrewd granddaughter."

"And you're a helluva grandma."

Naddy winked at her.

Alex tugged Naddy out of her seat and they went inside. Buck turned from stirring something on the stove. Connie was nowhere in sight.

He placed his hands on his hips, looking at Naddy. "Well, you found your way back."

"Yep."

Alex waited for the verbal warfare. There was nothing but absolute silence.

Buck was the first to speak. "I'm making spaghetti for supper. Anybody hungry?"

"Let me put my suitcase in my room and get out of these shoes," Naddy replied. "My dogs are barking."

As Naddy left, Alex folded her arms across her chest. "Where's Connie?"

"At her house, I suppose."

Alex thought it was time for a father-daughter talk. "Buck…"

"You didn't tell me Naddy was coming home."

He cut her off so fast she had whiplash. She realized they might never truly be open with one another. She realized something else, too—Buck still saw her as a little girl. That wouldn't change until she showed him she was an adult.

"I got the call and I responded. I didn't have time to let you know. Besides, I didn't think you cared."

He sprinkled seasoning into a pot. "It's always nice to know when a hurricane is coming."

Buck usually didn't have a sense of humor, but today he seemed different. Mellow even. So she jumped in with both feet.

"I'm going to start looking for an apartment."

"Should have done that years ago. Then Naddy wouldn't cling to you like a leech."

Not the response she expected, but at least he wasn't making her feel guilty about leaving.

"I'm worried about Naddy, though."

He swung around, his gray eyes hooded. "I told you Naddy can take care of herself, and you don't have to worry about me kicking her out. I won't."

"Okay. I'll start looking." Maturity in the Donovan house reached a new level. They were working things out. Alex felt excited about the future and being on her own.

For the first time the Donovans had supper together without tense verbal exchanges. Naddy pushed the edge of the envelope when she told Buck what had happened in Vegas.

It surprised Alex that Buck controlled his temper. He got up and carried dishes to the sink.

"Is he ill?" Naddy whispered to Alex.

Buck had heard her. "I'm not ill. It's time we started living our own lives and I'm through trying to raise you." He paused. "Alex is moving out."

"What!" Naddy turned to her, her eyes bright. "Are you moving in with a guy?"

"No." She shook her head. "It's time I was on my own."

"Hallelujah. It took you long enough. Ethel and me

will visit and give you tips on how to attract the opposite sex."

"I don't need any tips. Besides, you and Ethel are grounded."

"Honeychild, you can't ground someone older than you."

Alex lifted an eyebrow. "Really?"

"Well, maybe a little." Naddy stood with a grin. "Buck, the supper was good. You didn't learn how to cook from me. Now I better see if my computer's still working."

Alex helped Buck with the dishes.

"You weren't in the office today." Buck poured the remaining sauce into a container for the refrigerator. "Where were you?"

She leaned against the cabinet. "I was there for a little while. Claudia Hayes passed away last night."

Buck snapped a lid on the container. "That's a blow for your cowboy."

"Yeah. I'm caught in the middle of the Braxtons and Brodie."

"Get your heart out of the equation and you won't have a problem." He opened the refrigerator.

She told him about the other baby.

"Let the police handle it and get yourself back to work," was his response.

Buck believed in handling everything by the book, where there was no room for emotions.

She gritted her teeth and thought this was a good time to end the evening. Buck's blood pressure had been stable all night and she had a feeling it was about to explode like a can of Coke that had been left in the freezer.

Naddy was busy at her computer, her open, overflowing suitcase dumped on her bed. Life was back to normal. She trudged upstairs and fell across the bed. Should she let the police take over? She found she couldn't do that. Brodie had asked for her help and there was no way she'd let him down.

FIRST THING the next morning she called Brodie. It seemed so natural to talk to him before starting her day. They arranged to meet at Cleo's old house. Detective Crane and two of his guys were already there and had apprised the Simses of the situation the night before. Sueann took the children to her mother's, but she was soon back.

Brodie gave the detective the map Cleo had drawn. They stayed in the house while the police did their search. Sueann and her husband Ray sat staring at them. No one spoke.

"You look familiar," Ray said to Brodie. "I've seen you somewhere."

"I don't think we've met," Brodie replied.

"Brodie Hayes." Ray slapped his hand against his leg. "You're a bull rider. I've seen you ride."

Brodie's lips tightened. "That was years ago."

"Yeah, but you were one helluva bull rider."

"Thank you."

The stilted words sent Ray a message. Brodie didn't want to talk. Luckily the man received it loud and clear.

There was complete silence as they waited. Sueann offered them something to drink, but they refused. The burial had been so long ago Alex had her doubts about finding anything.

Mike finally came through the back door. Alex reached for Brodie's hand and he gripped it like a vise.

"Did you find anything?" Alex asked.

"It took a while, but we finally located the stones buried under the grass. And we located the remains wrapped in a blanket under the second stone." He held up a plastic bag. "You might be interested in this." Inside the bag was a tiny hospital identification band, parts of it still readable. It said, *Braxton Baby Boy* and there was a date, but it wasn't clear.

"She switched the bands," Brodie whispered.

"Looks like it," Mike agreed. "We're taking the remains to the lab."

"I'd…" Brodie swallowed visibly. "I'd like to have his remains buried with his mother."

Mike inclined his head. "Sure. After I get the paperwork done and get it cleared."

"You're not gonna leave my yard like that, are you?" Ray stared at his dug-up yard.

"No, Mr. Sims," Mike replied. "We'll put everything back just like it was."

"Good." Mr. Sims scratched his head. "Go figure. A baby buried in our backyard. Ain't that something."

"Who is this Braxton person?" Sueann asked.

"Someone who's been missing for a long time," Mike answered.

"Wow. Is it gonna be in the paper?"

"It's police business, Mrs. Sims, and I'd appreciate your discretion."

"Oh, sure."

Alex and Brodie walked to their vehicles in silence.

"Are you okay?" Alex asked.

"It was just like she said."

"Yes. Claudia didn't lie to you."

He looked off to the bright Texas sky. "I feel like I'm in someone else's dream, but I'm in someone else's life—for real. It's no dream."

"It's your life."

"We'll see." He turned toward his truck.

"Brodie…"

"I'm fine, Alex."

BRODIE DROVE to his mother's house. He now had one goal and he wasn't sure why it was so important to him.

"Brodie," Cleo said, anxious to see him. "What did they find?"

"The baby was buried there just like Mother said."

"Oh my God. How awful."

"Forensics has the remains now and they'll soon release it for burial."

As he walked toward the kitchen he saw a man he assumed was Melvin sitting at the table. Cleo introduced him and Brodie shook his hand.

"I'm so sorry about your mother," Melvin said.

"Thanks." He looked at Cleo. "Where did Mother keep all my baby stuff? I know she had a lot of it."

"I believe it's in that armoire in her bedroom. Why…?"

Brodie headed for the bedroom and opened the big double doors. A couple of boxes and several albums were in the bottom drawer. He carried everything to the bed. The albums chronicled his life from his birth to his college days. He looked closely at the photo of Claudia holding a baby in the hospital, then at the one of Tom holding his son in Germany. The babies looked the same.

He finally opened the box and went though his baby mementos, then he saw what he was looking for—his ID bracelet from the hospital. *Hayes Baby Boy*. This had to be buried with the baby who'd been dug up today. It belonged to him.

Staring at the albums on the bed, he felt that knot in his stomach again. The photos showed Brodie Hayes's life. But who was Brodie Hayes?

Chapter Twelve

The answer still eluded him as he drove home. Brodie was so bone-tired he didn't have enough strength left to face anything. He needed time alone to absorb what had happened in the last two days.

He had the urge to call Alex just to hear her voice. She was fun, exciting and she made him smile. Even when he was dealing with the worst pain of his life she had the ability to bring him down to earth with her red Popsicle tongue, her eccentric grandmother and her views on his truck.

The fact that she was in the enemy camp, as he thought of the Braxton family, kept him from picking up his cell phone. He felt, though, she was on his side, too. A thought from his pain-induced mind, he was sure. But he'd never met anyone like Alex Donovan before.

He spotted two trucks at his house and he recognized them immediately—Colter and Tripp. His friends met him halfway and they embraced, then walked together into the house.

"Marisa and Camila sent food. It's in the refrigerator," Tripp said.

"Thanks, but I'm not hungry."

"How about a beer?" Colter asked.

"Can always use a beer."

"Good." Tripp headed for the refrigerator.

"Not one 'I'm sorry' outta you guys," Brodie warned. "I heard too many in the last couple of days."

Tripp set beer on the table. "What can we do?"

"Nothing. There's nothing anyone can do."

"Tripp told me everything," Colter said.

Brodie pulled the tab on the beer can and took a big swallow. "I didn't want to tell you over the phone. Hell, it's hard to say the words out loud." He took a deep breath. "I'm not Brodie Hayes."

"Sure you are," Colter said. "You're the best damn bull rider who was ever born. You've got guts, grit, determination and a winning spirit in your soul. And you're a friend who would die for me. That's Brodie Hayes, the man I know."

"If the real Brodie Hayes was alive, he'd be in the military striving to achieve the rank of his father."

"You can't think that way," Tripp told him. "You didn't create this chaos, and sometimes a man has to be who he really is—that's why you're a bull rider."

"What the hell." Brodie shoved back his chair. "Let's ride like we used to when the world got us down." He headed for the door and the corrals.

They had the horses saddled in a matter of minutes and Brodie shot out of the barn, needing to ride like he'd never ridden before. He gave Jax his head and Tripp and Colter kept pace with him. They flew across pastures, scattering cattle, and sailed across a creek.

When he reached the second creek, he jumped from the saddle and ran to the water's edge, holding his arms wide. He felt as if the top of his head was about to explode like a rocket, spewing to the sky along with every dream, every emotion he'd ever felt.

Tripp and Colter dismounted, staring at him with worried expressions. The wind blew through the trees, rousing the heat to a fever pitch.

"Brodie…" Tripp moved toward him.

"How do you put a broken cowboy back together again?" he asked, hardly recognizing his own voice.

Neither Tripp nor Colter spoke.

"No answer?" he asked, his voice carrying on the wind.

"Well, I'm broken this time and there isn't enough tape in the world to hold me together." He squeezed his eyes shut. "I can't do this. I can't deal with the Braxton family. I can't be Travis Braxton."

Tripp and Colter walked to stand on either side of him. "Remember when you drew El Diablo to ride in the finals?" Colter asked.

"Yeah."

"He'd already mangled two cowboys and you said you couldn't do it."

"But you didn't back down," Tripp said, taking up the story. "You cowboyed up and rode him eight seconds and lived to tell about it."

"This is different."

"How?" Colter asked. "Just like El Diablo this is another unexpected twist in your life. You cowboy up and face it. Once a cowboy, always a cowboy. I've never known you to do anything else."

"Me, neither," Tripp added.

Brodie sucked in a breath of warm air and it flowed through his system like a wake-up call. He didn't have a choice. Like the draw in the rodeo, he had to face this situation. Or give up. Giving up wasn't in him though. He'd finally realized that.

He picked up his reins. *Time to cowboy up.*

They rode back to the house more slowly this time.

ALEX CALLED MIKE to make sure the ID bracelet did not go to the funeral home with the remains. She was sure Helen would want it.

She drove home and had a chat with Naddy and they worked out a payment schedule so she could repay Alex for the fine and damages. The talk went well and she planned to make Naddy keep her word.

Then she got a call from Ethel's daughter, who said Naddy was a bad influence on Ethel and would prefer if Alex kept Naddy away from her mother. This was one thing she didn't need today, but she tried to be as cordial as she could without being rude.

Naddy was at her computer and Buck was out. Alex munched on a Popsicle in the kitchen and wondered what Brodie was doing, and if he was alone. She hated the thought of him being alone. He probably wasn't. He had his aunt and his friends. But what if he was?

She threw the wrapper in the trash and grabbed her purse. "I'm going out, Naddy."

"Whatever."

She'd made so many trips to the Cowboy Up Ranch

that the Jeep could probably make it on its own. For her own peace of mind, though, she had to see him. She hoped he understood.

IT WAS AFTER nine when she drove into his yard. The big truck was there and a light was on inside the house. He was home—alone.

The dogs bounded from the barn and she took a moment to greet them, then she knocked at the door. There was no response so she knocked again.

Suddenly the door swung open. Brodie stood there in his bare feet, buttoning his shirt, which was out and over his jeans. His tousled hair and heavy eyes indicated he'd been sleeping.

"I'm sorry. I didn't mean to wake you."

He ran both hands over his face. "It's okay. I fell asleep in the chair. Lack of sleep is catching up with me."

"I…I…" It was hard to articulate what she was doing here this late.

He stepped aside. "Come in."

The house was in darkness except for a lamp in the den. She sat on the leather sofa and stared at an object on the coffee table. It was a baby's ID bracelet from the hospital. She tilted her head to read the name, but she didn't really have to. She already knew what it said.

Brodie eased into his chair, his eyes following her gaze. "My mother had all my baby things in a box and I picked up the bracelet earlier. I'll drop it by the funeral home in the morning."

She caught his eyes. "Brodie, you do realize you're not to blame for the baby's death?"

"Yes." He rubbed his hands together. "Somehow I have to do this. It makes it real for me and I can sort it out in my head."

"Good." She brushed a speck off her jeans. "Aren't you going to ask what I'm doing out here this time of night?"

"I don't even know what time it is." He stretched his arms above his head. The top buttons on his shirt were undone and she glimpsed the dark chest hairs against his sun-browned skin. Her stomach fluttered with awareness.

He lowered his arms and moved his shoulders in a tired way. "Have you got my place staked out?"

She'd love to stake him out day and night.

"No. I just wanted to see you." She surprised herself with the honest answer.

"From anybody else I'd take that as a come-on."

She blinked. What did that mean? He didn't see her as an attractive woman? Or he just wasn't interested?

"Are you hungry?"

The question caught her off guard and for a moment she was speechless.

He shoved to his feet. "Tripp and Colter were by earlier and Camila and Marisa sent food. I wasn't hungry then, but now I am. How about you?"

"Uh…yeah. I haven't had supper."

He strolled into the kitchen. "I have no idea what's in here. Camila's a great cook. Marisa's still learning."

She pulled out a chair and he brought food to the table. He laid a platter of sandwiches in front of her. "Peanut butter and jelly and ham and cheese. Marisa's handiwork because I've seen her make these for the kids, cutting the crust off the bread." He went back for more. "There's Camila's enchiladas and fruit and veggies. She's always trying to get me to eat healthy." He brought the fruit and veggies to the table. "Takes too long to heat up the enchiladas. Soft drink or beer?"

"Water, please."

He placed a cold bottle of water in front of her with a napkin, then straddled a chair, reaching for a sandwich. "Mmm. These are good."

"You like peanut butter and jelly?"

"You bet. My mother used to make…" His words trailed away as he realized what he was saying. "Claudia used to make them for me. Sometimes she'd make them into hearts, squares or circles."

"You can't erase a lifetime of memories," she told him.

"I sure wish I could."

She thought it best to change the subject. "You seem to have a good relationship with your friends' wives."

"Yeah." He picked up a slice of cantaloupe. "They're great women, but Colter's and Tripp's love didn't come without a price."

"What do you mean?"

"We met Marisa years ago in Vegas. She's from New York and a trained concert pianist. The moment she and Colter laid eyes on each other it was just like that." He snapped his fingers. "Instant attraction. He spent a lot of his winnings to buy her a ring."

"How romantic."

"Not quite. When Marisa's mother discovered where she was, she came to Vegas and forced Marisa to go home and back to her career. Colter was devastated."

"But she returned?"

"No. Not for nine years. You see, Marisa was pregnant when she left and her mother was furious. She wanted her to have an abortion. Marisa refused. Then she wanted her to give up the baby for adoption. Marisa wouldn't hear of it. She planned to keep the baby and find her way back to Colter."

Alex scooted to the edge of her chair, waiting with bated breath for his next words.

"Mrs. Preston had a plan, though. She had no intention of letting Marisa keep the baby. Marisa started having problems with the pregnancy and had to be hospitalized. Or at least she thought she was hospitalized. Mrs. Preston put her in an upscale home for unwed mothers and called Marisa's father, Richard Preston. They'd been divorced for a number of years but together they decided what was best for Marisa's life. When the baby was born, they told her the baby boy was stillborn."

"And they gave him away?" She couldn't keep the shock out of her voice.

"Yep."

"Oh, no."

"Don't get too upset. They hired a P.I. to find Colter and they made him an offer. If he wanted the baby, he could have her."

"Her?"

"Yes. The baby was really a girl. They only told Marisa it was a boy in case she ever saw Colter again. That way she wouldn't suspect a thing."

"And Colter took the baby?"

"Oh, yeah. He flew to New York and came back with

his baby girl. He was paranoid about that kid. We all tried to help him, but he insisted on doing everything for his child. She would never have a mother, but she would have a father who loved her."

"How did they meet again?" she asked.

"After losing her baby, Marisa couldn't play the piano anymore. She was distraught and Mr. Preston brought her home to Texas. She finally healed enough to go to college then she started working at Dalton Department Store headquarters."

"Oh. I finally made the connection. Richard Preston owns Dalton's."

"Yes. He's a powerful man and tried to run his daughter's life. He almost lost her."

"So how did they meet again?"

"Colter and Ellie, that's their daughter, were Christmas shopping in Dalton's and they ran into Marisa. Colter was angry and Marisa was hurt, wanting to tell him about the son who had died. Colter wanted nothing to do with her and he certainly didn't want her around Ellie."

"So Marisa didn't know Ellie was her daughter."

"No. It took a while for all the lies and deceit to unravel."

"Wow. What a story."

"Yeah. And it's still the same with them. Even in a crowded room sometimes all they see is each other."

"Now that's a fairy tale," she said, biting into a strawberry.

He popped a grape in his mouth. "You don't believe in that kind of love."

"Do you?"

"Colter got lucky—real lucky. After all the heartache, he's finally happy. I'm not sure that happens for everyone."

"What about Tripp? You've told me some of his story and he seems happy."

"Yeah, he's happy, too."

"We have about a dozen sandwiches to finish off so tell me more about Camila. What does she do?"

"As a teenage mom Camila devoted her life to raising Jilly. Jilly's almost fourteen now and known as the angel of Bramble, Texas."

"Really?"

"Yes. She spends all her time helping the elderly. She picks up their groceries, their medicine and just spends time with them when they're lonely."

"That's unusual."

"Camila did a super job raising her. Of course, Camila's a very good role model, very warm and loving. To stay at home with her daughter, Camila used her skills to create her own business, Camila's Common Threads."

"What's that?"

"She quilts, mostly baby quilts that she sells on the Internet and in her store. And she makes scented soaps, which seem to be very popular. They're sold all over Texas."

"She sounds very talented and creative."

"She is and she's also now the mayor of Bramble."

He talked so lovingly of these people and Alex knew they were his real family. The family that was always there for him.

She helped him put the food away.

"I've been talking too much."

"No. I loved hearing about your friends."

"If you come to the service, I'll introduce you."

"I'd like that."

He opened a drawer and pulled out a plastic bag. In the den, he dropped the bracelet into it. "I'll bring it to the funeral home first thing in the morning." He laid it on the coffee table and sat on the sofa, staring at it.

She sat beside him, hating to bring up something, but she had to. "I asked Mike to save the other bracelet for Mrs. Braxton. I'm sure she would want it."

"Probably."

"Brodie..."

"Alex, please. Don't tell me about them. If you do, they will become real. Right now, I can't handle any more reality."

"I know." She thought about the rattle and knew it wasn't the right time to give it to him. Slipping an arm around his waist, she rested against him. He pulled her closer, leaning back against the sofa. She could feel the steady beat of his heart. It was just the two of them, alone in this room. The world, the Braxtons, awaited outside. For tonight, though, there was just the moment and a cowboy who was hurting.

His hand slid to her hair and removed the clip, her blond hair tumbling to her shoulders. Cupping her head, he kissed her gently, then again, his lips barely touching hers yet it was the most powerful, erotic sensation she'd ever felt. His tongue ran across her bottom lip, tasting, tantalizing, then he kissed her deeply.

When she'd dreamed of kissing Brodie, it was

nothing like this—mind-tripping, spine-tingling good. It was like being without water for days and once you had that first sip, you couldn't get enough.

Her hand found its way inside his shirt and he caught it, kissing her knuckles, then her lips again briefly. Holding her close he reached up and turned off the lamp.

She curled into him, knowing that tonight the passion building between them would not find its release. He just needed someone to hold—to help him make it through the night so he could face tomorrow.

And that was a gift in itself—that he needed her.

Chapter Thirteen

Brodie woke up at dawn and stared down at the woman in his arms. Her head rested below his chin, her hand lay on his chest. She slept peacefully, making an occasional deep-breathing sound. That was probably as close to snoring as she would ever get.

It felt so right to have her in his arms. He'd never needed anyone in his life, but last night he'd needed her. It wasn't sexual, either. Not that he didn't want her. Last night was about something entirely different. It was about comfort, caring and mental nourishment so he could face another day. Holding on to Alex gave him that strength.

The pretty P.I. was getting to him and he didn't mind. Even though she worked for the Braxtons, he trusted her.

She stirred and sat up, brushing hair out of her eyes. "Good morning," she whispered.

He felt a catch in his gut at her sleep-filled voice. Her soft brown eyes were languid, sensuous, and he had a feeling she'd look like this after making love. After…

Rising to a sitting position, he flexed his shoulders. "Morning."

She sniffed the air. "I don't smell coffee. After spending the night on this sofa, I expected coffee to be brought to me." Her eyes twinkled.

"Yes, ma'am." He rose to his feet and headed for the kitchen. She had a knack for putting a smile on his face. When the first cup dripped out, he took it to her.

"Wonderful." She curled up in the corner of the sofa. "Yikes!"

"What?" He turned from getting himself a cup.

"This is black." She made a face and hurried after him to the kitchen.

"Oh. I forgot to ask. I'm not used to getting coffee for a woman."

"Really?" She put milk and sugar in her cup and stirred.

"Yes, really."

She leaned against the cabinet, sipping her coffee. "So I'm your first?"

He grinned. "So to speak."

"Cowboy, that is so hard to believe."

"Well, you see, I'm used to having a woman bring me coffee."

"Now that I believe." She smiled, bringing sunshine into the room.

He walked over and tucked her hair behind her ear, loving the easy banter between them. It's what he needed this morning. He needed her. "I'll bring you coffee any day of the week."

She looked at him over her cup. "I bet you get a lot of action with that response."

He placed a hand on either side of her. "Are you a taker?"

She twisted slightly to set her cup on the counter, then trailed a finger down his nose. "You have enough on your plate without adding another complication."

"Sex is never a complication."

"Oh, yeah." A bubbly laugh left her throat. "That's a man's point of view."

"Mmm." He caught her lips in a slow kiss. When she opened her mouth, he kissed her until he couldn't think. Only feel. And he was feeling her in ways…

"Whoa, cowboy." She rested her face in his neck. "We're getting sidetracked and you have a lot to do this morning."

"Yeah." He kissed her forehead. "Maybe later."

She drew back. "Maybe." She walked into the den and found her purse. "I'll see you at the service."

In a flash she was gone. Suddenly the gloom and doom of this day returned in full force. He took a moment and hurried to his bedroom.

ALEX WAS RUNNING LATE. Naddy and Buck had questions about where she was all night. Buck knew she wasn't working. For years she'd come and gone as she pleased, now all of a sudden she had two watchdogs on her case. She had to start looking for that apartment and soon.

She wanted to look nice so it took time choosing an outfit. She only had one black dress and debated whether to wear something else. In the end she wore the basic sleeveless, V-neck black dress with sandaled heels.

When she arrived, the small chapel was filling up with friends of the Hayes family. She saw Brodie in the front row with Tripp and a woman, whom she knew was his wife. Another couple sat beside them, which had to be Colter and his wife. Brodie's aunt was on his right.

While signing the guest book, she caught a glimpse out of the corner of her eye. She whirled around to face the Braxton family.

"What are you doing here?"

"I'm sorry, Alex," Helen said. "But we want to see him."

"I want to see my son," George added in a stubborn voice.

"This is not the time."

"I tried to tell them that, but they won't listen." Alex could see that Maggie had reached the end of her patience.

"Let him grieve for the woman who raised him," Alex said.

"You can't tell me what to do," George replied.

"Oh, yes, I can." Alex stood her ground. "If you confront him today, you will lose him for the rest of your life. Are you willing to chance that?"

"He's my son." George wiped away a tear and Alex felt a tug on her heart again at what these people had been through.

"I know, Mr. Braxton, but today is not the day to meet him."

"That's him, isn't it?" Helen was looking through the open doorway to the front row.

"Yes. That's Brodie Hayes."

Brodie stood to shake someone's hand. "He's so handsome."

"Go home, please. I'll be in touch."

Maggie took her father's arm. "Let's go, Dad."

He took one last look at Brodie and turned to leave.

"Mom," Maggie called.

Helen tore her eyes away and followed.

Alex let out a long breath and quickly took a seat in the back. The service had already started. The minister depicted a life of a general's wife who was devoted to her husband, her son and her numerous charities. The eulogy was nice and correct, no reference to the secret that the man in the front row would now have to face.

The service over, people stood to offer their condolences to Brodie and his aunt. She hesitated at the back, unsure whether to intrude on this private moment.

As the last person walked away, Brodie noticed her and motioned for her to come forward. She made her way to the front thinking how great he looked in the dark navy suit.

Brodie quickly made the introductions of his friends and aunt. "Nice to meet you," she said, shaking hands.

They smiled and responded in kind, putting her at ease. Marisa was as fair as Camila was dark and both were very friendly. Since she'd heard their stories, she felt as if she knew them.

A man from the funeral home came up to Brodie and whispered something to him.

"They'll be ready to leave for the airport in ten minutes."

"I'll bring the car around," Colter said, grabbing his hat from the pew.

"We'll all go, so we'll be in the vehicle ready to follow the hearse." Tripp reached for his hat.

Marisa and Camila said goodbye and Brodie and Alex stood alone.

"How are you?" she asked. The blue eyes were sad and her heart contracted.

He touched her cheek and it felt as warm as the August heat. "You ask me that all the time."

"I'm worried about you."

"Mmm." He nodded. "I don't believe anyone has worried about me so much before."

They stared at each other, lost in the new feelings developing between them.

The funeral director spoke to Brodie and he had to speak twice before Brodie heard him.

"I've got to go," Brodie said, bending down for his hat. "After the burial at Arlington, we're flying back tonight. It'll be late, but…"

"I'll see you then."

He settled his hat on his head. "Later."

As he walked away, she watched him for a moment then made her way to the back of the funeral home. She crawled into her Jeep and waited as the hearse pulled away with a Suburban behind it. She was glad his friends were going with him.

SHE WENT HOME, changed and headed for the police station. Mike had the bracelet waiting for her. She made a quick stop by her office to get the directions to the Braxton ranch.

As she was going through the Braxton file, Buck walked in. "You finally showed up for work."

"Not really. I'm only here for a minute."

"Now listen, girl. We have a lot of work to do. And I took on a new case. Danny Davis is serving time for a crime his mother says he didn't commit. I'll need your help digging though all the court transcripts and documents."

"Sure." She pulled out the directions Helen had given her. "But not for a couple of days."

"What! Why not?"

"I'm busy on something else."

He shook his head. "You just never learn."

She got to her feet. "Buck…"

"Let the cowboy handle his own affairs. You're getting too involved."

"I tore his world apart and now I have to be there for him…and the Braxtons."

"Are you even aware of a P.I.'s job description?" His voice rose and she refrained from gritting her teeth. "Collect the facts, deliver them, get paid and get the hell out."

She reached for her purse. "That's the difference between you and me. I can't turn my back when someone is hurting."

"Holy Moses. Joan branded you for life."

"And you're never going to change that in me. I'm more like my mother than you, so deal with it." She slung her purse over her shoulder, finally realizing and accepting that that trait in her personality was never going to change. That's who she was. "Catch you later."

THE DRIVE TO Weatherford was long and tedious on the freeway. The town of about twenty thousand people was located sixty miles west of Dallas and was mostly a farming and ranching community. Weatherford was known as the cutting horse capital of the world. Horse ranches dotted the landscape. Since it was summer, the pastures had a parched looked. Those that had irrigation were greener.

She turned off I-30 and followed the directions. Soon she saw the county road listed and made another turn. The Braxton ranch came into sight—Lazy B Horse Farm.

Beneath an oak tree a couple of horses munched on grass. The white limestone ranch house had a long front porch and a chain-link fence enclosed the yard. Barns and pens were in the distance. There was a feeling of neglect about the place. The fences had barbed wire broken or missing and weeds grew wild around the barn and in the pastures.

As she got out she noticed everything was quiet and she wondered if anyone was home. Or maybe that's just the way it was in the country. She'd called Helen to let her know she was coming so they should be here.

A reddish-brown cocker spaniel jumped from the porch and crawled beneath the fence to greet her. After a couple of barks, the front door opened and Helen came out.

"Come in, Alex," Helen called.

She opened the gate and walked up the paved walk, the dog following her.

"Don't mind Daisy. She's not much of a guard dog."

On the porch, they stood face-to-face and Alex could see the pain in Helen's eyes. "I hope I'm not intruding."

"No, dear. What's this about?"

"I'd like to speak with you about Brodie."

Helen sighed. "Alex, we can't take much more. I'm sorry about this morning, but we had to see him."

"I know. But my visit is about something else."

Maggie came to the door. "Come in, Alex. It's too hot to be standing out there."

Alex walked into a country-style home with over-stuffed tweed furniture, two recliners, oak paneling and a braided rug covering hardwood floors. George sat in one of the recliners.

"What do you want?" he asked, his voice unfriendly.

"I know this is hard…"

"Please have a seat," Maggie said.

She sat on the sofa, hoping to explain, or at least take away some of their pain. "I'd like to tell you what's happened in the last few days."

"Would you like a glass of tea?" Maggie asked.

"No. Thank you."

Helen took a seat beside her. "What's happened?"

She told them the story of digging up the Hayes baby.

"So she buried her dead baby?" Helen asked.

"Yes."

"And stole mine?"

"Yes."

"The police already called us, but it doesn't concern us. That's not our baby. He's still alive."

"Yes, he is, but you don't know the effect this is having on Brodie. It's almost too much for him to take, and he's a strong man. He wanted the baby to be with his mother so the baby is also being buried at Arlington National Cemetery."

"Why are you telling us this?" George wanted to know.

"So you'll understand his reticence and not be hurt by it. And I thought you might want this." She reached into her purse and pulled out the bracelet. "It was found wrapped with the remains." She handed the plastic bag to Helen.

She stared down at it and tears began to roll down her cheeks. "Oh, my. Oh, my."

"What is it?" George asked.

Helen got up and showed the decaying bracelet to him. His hand shook as he touched it.

"Mrs. Hayes switched the ID bracelets. Travis Braxton became Brodie Hayes that night." Alex paused. "He still is Brodie Hayes and probably always will be."

"No, he isn't," George shouted.

Alex exhaled a deep breath. "Mr. Braxton, you can't turn back the clock. I wish I could. There has to be some give-and-take for this to work out. You can't expect Brodie to be Travis Braxton just like that." She snapped her fingers. "And Brodie can't expect you to forget about him. Somewhere there has to be a compromise."

There was complete silence.

"What do you want us to do?" Helen finally asked.

"Let me continue to talk to him. Once he puts Mrs. Hayes's death behind him, I think he'll be more open to discuss the future."

"Okay. That's what we'll do," Helen said. "I've already seen him so I can wait a little longer."

Maggie walked Alex to the door. "Thank you for being so patient with them."

"I know they're hurting and I'm so hoping that this has a happy ending."

"Me, too." Maggie gave a slight smile. "My twelve-year-old son, Cody, can't believe Brodie Hayes is his uncle. He wants to tell everyone in school, but I told him we had to wait."

"That's probably wise."

Alex drove away feeling good about the visit. Brodie would have some time to think and get his life into perspective before the Braxtons confronted him. She was hoping he'd make the right decision.

THE TRIP WAS about an hour, but the traffic was heavy so it took longer. She finally pulled into her driveway, turned on the sprinklers and ran inside.

Naddy grabbed her as soon as she came through the back door, and swung her around. "Hallelujah. I just hit the jackpot."

Alex caught her forearms. "Calm down. What are you talking about?"

Naddy held a hand to her chest and collapsed into a chair. "Heavens. I'm too old to be going in circles. My head's spinning."

"What's all the excitement about?"

Naddy's gray eyes grew big. "You're not going to believe this. The dead girl in Vegas is the girl that went missing fourteen years ago."

"Wow. That's great work."

"You bet it is, honeychild. There was a twenty-five-thousand-dollar reward for any information that might lead to finding her. Didn't even know that, but I got a call a little while ago from a detective and he said the family's attorney would be in touch. Man, I've hit the jackpot. Ethel and me are going to Atlantic City." Naddy charged toward her bedroom.

"Wait a minute." Alex caught up with her. "You're *not* going to Atlantic City and you're *not* blowing twenty-five grand."

"Says who?"

"Me. You owe me a chunk of it and we'll budget the rest, so much a month."

Naddy shook her head. "You're such a spoilsport but I know you can't help it. You're Buck's daughter."

They heard the back door open and knew it was Buck. Naddy quickly regaled her son with her story. Buck responded the same way that Alex had.

He pointed a finger at Naddy. "You're not spending every dime of that."

"Bucky boy, I could be dead tomorrow so I'm living while I can."

Alex headed for the stairs, letting them fight it out. But she was beginning to think that Naddy might have the right idea—live life to the fullest because tomorrow was always a gamble.

WHEN SHE CAME DOWNSTAIRS, Buck was alone in the kitchen. Naddy's door was closed.

"Crazy old woman," Buck muttered.

Alex got a Popsicle out of the freezer. "Yeah. But it's her money. I'm sure the family is relieved knowing what happened to their daughter. Maybe now they can put her to rest." Alex picked up her purse, thinking about the case that had caused her to leave the police force. Those parents had put their daughter to rest. Alex wouldn't change anything she'd done on that case. She'd put her heart into it and she would again. That was just her.

"Where're you going?" Buck asked.

"Out."

"To see the cowboy?"

"Maybe."

"Girl, why can't you let this go?"

She peeled the paper off the Popsicle and thought she'd be honest with Buck…and herself.

"I think I'm in love with him."

Chapter Fourteen

Alex left Buck with his mouth open—for once he had nothing to say. Just as well. She wasn't sure she would have wanted to hear his reaction. Nevertheless, she'd wanted to share her feelings with her father. Maybe she needed to hear the words out loud. This was a wonderful feeling she'd discovered, and Alex felt like shouting it from the rooftops.

She drove through the hot night, headed for Brodie's ranch. He wouldn't be home yet, but she wanted to be there when he returned. The drive gave her time to think about love and how, when it was right, a woman knew. From the first moment Brodie stepped out of his truck something happened inside her. Her pulse leaped, her palms were sweaty, and her heart knew that Brodie Hayes was special.

Through the weeks that followed the way she felt hadn't changed, except now she recognized her emotions for what they were. Brodie was the part of her she'd been searching for—the missing part that made her complete.

Buck might laugh at that, but Alex believed in love, and she believed in happily ever after. It didn't matter what Buck thought. Only Brodie mattered. She wasn't sure he felt the same about her, but she would be there for him, though—no matter what.

She parked and got out. Away from Dallas the night air wasn't so stifling. The dogs appeared out of nowhere and she sat on the step, petting them. Leaning back against the door, Alex waited.

BRODIE COULDN'T WAIT for the plane to touch down. This day would always be etched in his memory—the day he said goodbye to the woman who'd raised him. The woman who wasn't his mother. So why did it still feel as if she had been?

With no luggage to wait for it didn't take them long to get through the airport. Colter drove them to the funeral home to pick up Brodie's truck. They said goodbye and he knew Colter and Tripp were worried about him. Hell, he was worried about himself. Right now it didn't feel as if he'd ever recover from this ordeal.

He took Cleo to his mother's house. Flipping on a light, he asked, "Are you going to be okay?"

"Sure." Cleo laid her purse on the sofa. "Melvin will be over in the morning."

"That's good. You won't be alone."

She fingered her beads. "Melvin asked me to move in with him before Claudia passed, but I couldn't because Claudia needed me. Now I'm thinking about doing it."

"You're welcome to stay here as long as you want."

She shrugged. "It's not the same without Claudie."

"Whatever you want to do is fine with me."

She gave him a hug. "I feel so bad that this happened to you."

He tried to smile and failed. "Heck. I'm tough. I'm a bull rider. I'll get through this."

"I just want you to be happy—like your friends."

"I don't think that's possible."

She hugged him again. "Be happy, Brodie."

He kissed her cheek and went to his truck, totally drained of every emotion. It was time to go home, to find some sort of peace.

THE BEAM OF his headlights picked out the Jeep parked in his yard. Alex was here. Suddenly he wasn't so tired anymore. Getting out he saw her sitting on the step, sound asleep, the dogs keeping guard.

It was after twelve. How many women would wait in the darkness all alone? Alex was one of a kind. He eased himself down to sit beside her.

Startled, she jumped straight up.

"It's just me."

"Oh." She pushed her hair out of her eyes. "You scared me."

"Sorry. Didn't mean to do that."

She plopped next to him and he pulled her into his arms. Being with her felt as natural as breathing.

"How was your day?" she asked.

"Awful. Tiring. Claudia and Brodie Hayes are now with Thomas, the way it should be. But I'm still here. I'm trying to make sense of that."

"You will. You just need time."

"Maybe."

She rubbed her head against him. "It's so peaceful out here."

"And very warm."

"Mmm, I hardly noticed."

He cupped her face and kissed her. She tasted of strawberries and he smiled. "You've been eating a Popsicle."

"Guilty." She ran her tongue along his lower lip and his loins tightened with an uncontrollable urgency. Tonight he needed her in another way—the way a man needs a woman.

He kissed her deeply as the intensity of their emotions surrounded them. "Alex." He kissed her nose, her cheek, and nibbled on her ear. "I want you. If that's not what you want, let's stop now."

"I'm not stopping, cowboy." He could feel her smile.

He stood and unlocked the door. Inside, he flipped on a light, but all he wanted to see was her soft brown eyes. Taking her hand, they walked to the bedroom.

Sitting on the bed, the moonlight streaming through the window, he drew her between his legs. "This time I want to be awake when you take off my boots."

She removed his hat and tossed it into a corner. "I'd like for you to be awake during the whole thing."

"Deal." He slipped her tank top over her head and unsnapped her bra. Her skin was smooth, silky, heavenly. Her breasts spilled into his hands. He took his time getting acquainted with each one, caressing, stroking with his tongue. She moaned a sensuous sound and he reached up to take her lips. They fell backward onto the bed.

She quickly kicked off her sneakers and slid out of her jeans. He held her naked skin against him. But it wasn't enough. He had too many clothes on.

Sensing his need, she tugged on his boots until they were off, then she leaned over him. "I always wanted to undress a cowboy."

"Will any cowboy do?" he breathed into her neck.

"One with a big old truck." A gurgle of laughter erupted from her throat.

"I'm your man."

"Mmm." She slowly unbuttoned his dress shirt and slipped it from his shoulders. Her lips trailed down his chest to his belt buckle and every need jerked alive inside him. He shimmied out of his pants and they were skin on skin, heart on heart. She was as soft as he was hard. His mouth tasted every inch of her, from her lips to the tips of her toes. He didn't leave any place untouched.

"Brodie," she moaned on a ragged breath. Taking the initiative, her lips began a thorough search of his body. He caught her head and pulled her up to him.

"I need you...now."

"Condom?"

He fumbled in the nightstand until he found one and quickly sheathed himself.

"You do that so well." She growled deep in her throat.

"Practice makes perfect."

She tugged on his chest hairs. "That's not something you should tell me right now."

"Oh, Alex, sweet Alex." He took her lips hungrily, wrapping his arms around her.

Alex felt as if she'd died and gone to heaven. His

touch sensitized every part of her and she wanted all of him, totally, completely.

Her hand slid down his body, loving the texture of his skin, his hardness and his masculinity. She massaged and stroked until he flipped her onto her back.

"You're driving me crazy." His voice was a husky whisper. "I want you—now."

His lips captured hers as he thrust into her. She lost it then, wildly meeting his thrusts, clawing his back on a ride of pure undiluted pleasure. Her body convulsed into an orgasmic awakening.

She held him as he trembled his release. Breathing heavily, he rolled away and pulled her to him. Kissing his chest, she knew she'd never had sex like this before. She wanted to tell him how she felt, but it was the wrong time.

I love you, Brodie Hayes.

Nestling against him, she drifted into sleep and dreams of happily ever after.

BRODIE WOKE UP feeling relaxed for the first time in weeks. He pulled Alex closer, just savoring this moment with her. She'd saved him and now he was ready to face the future—whatever that might be.

Alex stirred and raised her head. "Morning, cowboy."

She looked just like he knew she would, her eyes dark and dreamy.

"Morning," he replied, grinning. She reached up and kissed his dimple, then her lips met his.

"Mmm." He kissed her deeply. "This is a nice way to wake up."

She slid her leg across his hip and straddled him.

"This is even better. Who knew the lady P.I. was cool on the outside, but wild in bed."

She pushed back her hair with both hands. "Was I wild?"

"You were magnificent."

She frowned. "I'm not usually."

"Usually?" He lifted an eyebrow. "Have there been many usuallys?"

She looked down at him, her eyes bright. "I can count them on one hand minus a couple of fingers." She inched a finger down his chest. "How about you, cowboy?"

"I don't have enough fingers," he replied and couldn't stop the grin that spread across his face.

"I thought so. I mean a man who keeps condoms in his nightstand, well…" She let out a shriek as he rolled her onto her back.

But you will be my last, he thought as his mouth covered hers and they forgot everything but this moment and each other.

AN HOUR LATER Alex sat at the kitchen table in Brodie's shirt. He'd fixed breakfast and she sipped coffee, not wanting this time to end.

"I guess I should get dressed and head back to the city."

Brodie wore nothing but his jeans and her senses spun at just the sight of his broad shoulders and bare chest.

"Do you have to go to work?"

"Not really."

"Then stay the day. I'll show you the ranch." He took a swallow of coffee. "Do you ride?"

"You bet, but I haven't in a long time."

He shoved back his chair. "Let's get dressed. I'll put the dishes in the dishwasher while you're dressing." He carried plates to the sink. "If I go with you, we'll probably never leave the house and I really need to check my cattle."

"Give me five minutes—tops."

In fifteen minutes, they were at the barn, the dogs following behind. Brodie gave her a hat and she put it on, feeling more and more like a cowgirl. Since it was early the heat wasn't so bad, but the sun would be scorching later. She waited while he went to get the horses. He led two inside.

"This is Star. She's a gentle mare."

"Oh." She stroked the horse's face. "You think I need gentle?"

"Yep. Until I know how you can ride." He swung a saddle onto Star's back.

He showed her how to gird the saddle tight and she listened avidly. They turned as they heard the pounding of hooves. A young boy rode into the barn.

"Hey, Brodie. You're back." He jumped from the saddle.

"Hey, Joey," Brodie said. "Thanks for looking after the ranch."

"No problem. I did everything you told me and made sure there was plenty of water in all the troughs." Joey kept staring at her.

"This is Alex Donovan." Brodie made the introduction. "And this is Joey, who hasn't learned all his manners yet."

"Oh. I'm sorry. I didn't mean to stare, but you're so pretty." His face turned a bright red.

"Thank you, Joey. It's nice to meet you."

"Ah...ah...yeah." He quickly swung back into the saddle. "I better go. 'Bye." He rode away.

"He's a little shy."

"But a fan of Brodie Hayes?"

"Sort of." He pulled Star forward. "Let's ride, lady."

Alex hadn't been in the saddle for a while, but she adjusted quickly. The ranch covered many acres. The land was very flat with a couple of creeks running through it. Some pastures had been cleared to make hay fields. Others had towering oak trees with green coastal growing beneath them. Red-faced cattle grazed contentedly.

"What kind of cattle are those?" she asked as they rode through a herd.

"Hereford."

They checked several water troughs to make sure the water was flowing. Brodie dismounted at a windmill and looked things over. She glanced up at the huge blades turning in the wind, creating energy to pump the water. Water was vital to a rancher—even she knew that.

At midday Brodie stopped by a slow-flowing creek. A large oak's branches hung over the water. "Ready for a break?"

"Sure."

He pulled a blanket from his saddlebags and spread it beneath the tree. She flopped down searching for ants and other critters. He handed her a canteen.

"What's this?"

"Water. Don't want to get dehydrated out here in the heat. And I have peanut butter crackers."

"I love a man who's prepared." She took a swig.

"I'm always prepared."

"Yes. I know." She gave him the canteen. "Are there any condoms in that bag?"

He lifted an eyebrow. "Do you want to find out?"

She suppressed a laugh. "Not here in broad daylight. Maybe later."

Leaning back against the tree, he opened the crackers and handed her one. She munched on it and just enjoyed the serenity of the outdoors…and Brodie. Sweat rolled down her back and saturated her waistline. She didn't care. She'd never been so happy in her life.

"Is it always this quiet?"

"Pretty much. Unless we're herding cattle—then things get lively."

They sat together for a while in a comfortable silence. The horses munched on grass and the dogs lay in the shade.

"You haven't said much about yesterday," she finally said.

He plucked a blade of grass. "Not much to say. I'm just glad it's over."

"Are you still having conflicting thoughts?"

"I buried Brodie Hayes yesterday. Now I'm trying to figure out who I'm supposed to be."

She took a deep breath. "You probably won't be able to do that until you speak with the Braxtons."

He didn't offer a protest like he usually did. He just stared off to the landscape.

So she plunged in. "Their names are George and Helen and you were their firstborn. You're named after him—George Travis Junior. Maggie, your sister, has two children, Amber and Cody. Cody's excited that his uncle is Brodie Hayes. I believe he loves rodeos."

Brodie didn't speak or try to stop her, so she continued. "The Braxtons have had a lot of heartache in their lives. They had two other sons, Will and Wesley, who both died. Will drowned when he was nineteen, and Wes died just last year in a car accident. George sank into deep depression after that, which is part of the reason I think Helen began her search for you again in earnest. Seeing your photo in the paper fueled her hopes. You're her only remaining son. She needed a miracle to save her sanity, her family. And she got one."

Brodie remained silent.

"George and Helen raise cutting horses in Weatherford. Or at least they used to. When Wes died, George sold all the horses except a few. He had no desire to continue working or living. They live on a ranch that's been in the family for years, but now it's in dire neglect. They…"

Brodie jumped up and grabbed the reins of his horse. "I need to check some fences."

He swung into the saddle and she quickly followed. He wasn't getting away from her. They rode until Alex was one big sweat gland and her body ached all over.

Brodie's face was set, his jaw clenched. She could see the muscle working in his neck and she knew he was trying to deal with everything she'd told him.

They kept riding, stopping only for water. And she began to wonder if he would ever tire. As the sun began to sink in the west, Brodie made his way back to the creek.

"I forgot the blanket," he said.

She dismounted with a moan and fell prone on her

stomach to the blanket. "I'm sorry, but I need a minute." She might be a wimp, but she'd kept pace with him as long as she could.

He squatted and began to remove her sneakers.

She flipped over. "What…"

"The creek water is cool. It'll rejuvenate you."

"That might take more than cool water."

He effortlessly slipped off his boots and removed his socks. Rolling up his jeans, he said, "Come on."

She quickly shed her shoes and socks. The ground was hard and dry beneath her feet, but the water was oh, so cool. Even the mud squishing between her toes felt wonderful.

"This is heavenly. I want to submerge my whole body."

"Go ahead. The water is deeper over here."

It was almost twilight and the place was in the middle of nowhere. What the hell. She removed her clothes and threw them on the bank. Brodie did the same. Together they sank beneath the cool surface.

They came up laughing and splashing each other. The tension of the day seemed to melt away. After a moment Brodie swung her up in his arms and carried her to the blanket. He fished a condom out of his jeans and she burst out laughing, kissing his dimple, his neck, his chest and lower.

They made slow, sweet love and the experience was better than the night before. Maybe it was the night, the heat or just the two of them needing each other.

Later they dressed and sat together, his arms locked around her. He nuzzled her hair. "Call the Braxtons. I'll meet them."

Chapter Fifteen

Alex could hardly contain her excitement. It had been a difficult decision, but she knew he'd made the right one.

That night she gave him the baby rattle. He stared at it a long time, then put it away in a drawer. He didn't say anything and she didn't press for a response.

At dawn she left to make the arrangements. She gave him a long kiss, knowing their special time had come to an end. She also knew it wasn't really an end, but a new beginning.

Buck was drinking coffee and reading the paper when she came through the door. He laid it down when he saw her.

"You just now gettin' home?"

She needed her own place—desperately.

"Yes, Buck, and good morning to you, too."

He frowned. "What's wrong with your hair?"

"It got wet." She'd washed it in Brodie's shower, but he didn't give her time to do anything with it. It hung in rattails around her face.

"It hasn't rained."

She rolled her eyes. "I have to change."

"You helping with the Davis case today?" he called after her.

"Probably not."

"Girl…"

After slamming her door, she didn't hear anything else. She picked up the phone and called the Braxtons. They were ecstatic, just as she knew they would be. She arranged a meeting for one o'clock. This was a new beginning for the Braxtons and Brodie. She prayed it went well.

In thirty minutes she was back in the kitchen. Buck was still at the table.

"You need to do something about Naddy."

She poured a cup of coffee. "Why?"

"She's making plans for that money, even though she hasn't gotten it yet."

"There's nothing wrong with that."

"She ordered a hot tub and the company was all set to deliver it. I canceled the damn order. And she's trying to trade in the Buick. The last thing she needs is a faster car. The old bat is losing her mind."

As she sipped her coffee, Alex wondered what Buck was so afraid of. There was a definite tone of fear in his voice. Then it hit her. He liked having Naddy under his thumb. It was the way things had always been between them and he was afraid of change. And he was afraid of losing his mother. Or maybe she had her rose-colored glasses on this morning. Or it could be that she was in love and she now saw the world differently.

"I'll talk to Naddy."

"Did I hear my name?" Naddy walked in looking like

something out of a scary movie. Her hair stuck out in all directions and her makeup was smeared, her eyeliner running in trails down her cheeks. Evidently she'd gone out shopping yesterday and had forgotten to remove her war paint.

Naddy pointed a finger at Buck. "You can badmouth me all you want, but I'm gettin' a hot tub."

"Not on my patio." He slapped the paper onto the table. "The last thing the neighbors need is to see you in a bathing suit."

Naddy placed her hands on her hips. "Who said I was going to wear one?"

Buck's mouth fell open and Alex set down her cup. "I'm outta here." She kissed Naddy's cheek. "Wash your face. I'll talk to you later."

"Oh. Okay."

Alex smiled all the way to her car. Backing out of the drive, she made a decision. It was time to stop telling herself to get a life and to get one. She stopped at a real estate office and asked to see some apartments.

Within the hour, she'd signed a lease. The agent kept trying to show her more apartments, but she liked the third one she looked at—a two-bedroom on a ground floor with a view of a large pool. The apartments were new and the extra bedroom would be nice if Buck kicked Naddy out. The pool might take her mind off the hot tub.

She immediately recognized what she was doing with that thought—clinging to those ties of family. But she would never abandon Naddy.

She stopped for a quick bite and wondered what Brodie was doing. Even though he was nervous, he wouldn't back out of the meeting. She couldn't wait to see him. They'd been apart too long.

As she parked her Jeep in her spot, she noticed his truck was already there. Why was he so early? The Braxtons weren't due for another thirty minutes. Maybe he missed her, too.

She hurried inside and found him pacing in her office. "Hi," she said, throwing her purse on her desk. "You're early." She went into his arms and he gripped her tightly.

"Thought I'd have a few minutes with you first."

She drew back. "These people have been waiting forever to see you. Just relax."

"I hope they don't expect too much. I'm just trying to get through this."

"Brodie..."

They heard the front door open. The Braxtons were early, too. Brodie stiffened and she didn't know how to help him. She gave him a quick kiss then went to meet the Braxtons.

"Is he here?" Helen asked, eager as a child.

"Yes. He's in my office. Let's just take it slow."

BRODIE WAITED with his breath wedged in his throat like a piece of barbed wire. After hearing their story, he couldn't in good conscience continue to refuse to see them. They were victims in this drama, just as he was.

An older woman of medium height with graying brown hair and green eyes came in first. A man and younger woman stood behind her. Tears filled the woman's eyes when she saw him.

"You're my son."

He removed his hat. "I believe so, ma'am."

"This is your father, George, and your sister, Maggie."

"Nice to meet you." The knot in his stomach was so tight he had trouble breathing.

George stepped forward. "I thought I'd never live to see this day. You're my boy. The one who was stolen from the hospital."

"Yes, sir," Brodie replied, staring at the gray-haired man. He saw his own features reflected in the man's face and he knew that in the years ahead, he would look just like this man—his father. It was a startling revelation.

Something clicked in his head and the link that tied him to Thomas and Claudia Hayes weakened. The Braxtons were real. Their blood ran through his veins. He was on the verge of finding a part of himself—the part that had been missing for so many years.

"Did Alex give you the baby rattle?" Helen asked.

"Yes. Thank you."

"I've had it since you were born."

Brodie didn't know what to say. When Alex had given it to him, it had meant nothing and he felt bad about that. But seeing the hope in Helen's eyes he knew it meant a lot to her.

"I always wondered what you looked like," Helen went on. "You look the same as George as a young man."

"People said I looked like my father, Thomas Hayes." The words came out before he could stop them.

"He's not your father," George shouted.

Maggie clutched his arm. "Dad, please."

"I'm sorry," George apologized. "I'm a little emotional."

"I am, too," Brodie said. "And I'm feeling overwhelmed so please give me time to adjust."

"Sure." Helen walked closer. "We know that you're grown, but we just want to be a part of your life."

"I'm not sure what that is at the moment."

"Mom, Dad, I think we need to go," Maggie said.

"Okay." But Helen hesitated. "Maybe you'll come for Sunday dinner. I make a pot roast that all my kids love."

"I'll think about it," was all he could say. He saw the hurt in her eyes, but he felt powerless to change that. He needed to do things at his own pace.

Maggie scribbled something on a piece of paper and handed it to him. "Here are our phone numbers and address, just in case you feel the need to visit."

"Thank you."

Helen looked at him. "Do you mind if I hug you?"

He swallowed hard, knowing if she touched him, it would change him forever. But he felt powerless to stop that, too.

"No," he muttered.

Her arms went around his waist and she clung to him, his shirt soaking up her tears.

"Mom." Maggie gently pulled her away.

The trio walked out and he had to take several deep breaths. Alex moved toward him and he gripped her with arms that trembled.

"It went well," she said.

He drew back. "I have to get out of here." He fled from the office.

"Brodie." Alex ran after him, but the white truck was already backing out. She would let him go—for now.

Buck walked in with a box of files. "Close the door," he ordered. "You're letting out all the cool air."

She closed the door with a sinking feeling in her stomach.

"I need your help with these files," Buck said. "So park your butt in a chair and get to work."

She spent the rest of the afternoon helping Buck on the Davis case, but her thoughts were never far from Brodie.

BRODIE DID WHAT he always did when the world closed in on him. He saddled up. When he rode, there were no doubts, no insecurities. He was in control completely and he needed to feel that way today—to have some sort of reality.

But as hard as he rode, he couldn't escape the reality he'd met today—his biological parents. The pain and grief in their eyes was impossible to ignore. That was his fault—he was the cause of that pain.

As the sun sank in the distant horizon, he made his way back to the barn, letting Jax take his time. He couldn't outride the demons chasing him. He had to face them.

In the barn, he unsaddled his horse and rubbed him down. Opening the gate to the pasture, he saw headlights coming down the road. He knew who it was. Alex.

He quickly strolled toward the house and she met him halfway. "How are you?" she asked.

"I'd feel a lot better with my arms around you."

"You got it, cowboy." She went into his arms and he held her tight, loving the lavender scent of her hair, the softness of her body. But most of all he just loved… He stilled as the truth made itself known. *He loved her.* The realization was overwhelming. This was something he never thought would happen to him. His love had grown out of her caring and loving nature. But was it real? Or was it something he needed to cling to because of all of the problems in his life?

What was he doing? He had no right to drag her into his messed up world.

"Brodie?" She looked up at him.

He should end it now before she got hurt. He had nothing to offer her, not even a name. But she'd asked nothing of him and he found he couldn't do the right thing. He still needed her. He might hate himself in the morning, but tonight he was going to love her like there was no tomorrow.

He looped an arm around her waist and they walked to the house. Inside he took her into his arms and kissed her with a hunger he didn't disguise, then he led her to the bedroom.

THEIR LOVEMAKING was intense and wild, born out of a need to find comfort in each other. A long time later their sweat-bathed bodies lay entwined. Alex was relaxed and sated to the point that all she wanted to do was sleep. But they had to talk.

She rose to a sitting position. "Feel better?"

"Yep." He reached up to touch her breast. "Your kisses are better than the kick I get from that first cup of coffee in the morning. And making love with you is better than any eight-second ride I've ever accomplished."

"Wow. Those are some powerful words."

"I mean them."

As much as she wanted to get lost in what he was saying, she couldn't. There were so many things they needed to discuss.

She stroked his chest. "Let's talk."

"I'd rather not."

"Please. For me."

He turned onto his side, his head propped in his hand. "What do you want to talk about?"

"Today."

"Today I saw all their pain. It was almost more than I could stomach, but I just couldn't undo forty years. I couldn't be their son."

"It will take time."

"I'm not so sure I'll ever be ready to be their son."

She curled her legs beneath her, trying to figure out what was really bothering him. Then she knew what it was.

"It's all right to be angry."

"What do you mean?"

"It's all right to be angry with Claudia. Ever since you found out you haven't allowed yourself to be angry at her."

"Didn't see the need."

"But you're angry. Admit it."

He scooted up to the headboard, but didn't say anything.

"Admit that you're angry."

"Okay," he snapped. "I'm angry. She took me out of that hospital uncaring about what she was doing to me and that family. She just wanted a child because she knew Thomas would blame her for the death of his son.

For years I lived with a knot in my gut because I couldn't be the son they wanted me to be. Finally, I couldn't take the pressure anymore and I bolted for some peace of mind." He dragged his hands over his face. "How could she do that to me? To that family?"

"Because she wasn't in her right mind."

"I know," he murmured.

There was complete silence.

"Now forgive her. Really forgive her."

"What?" He turned his head toward her. The room was in darkness, except for the moonlight and she couldn't see his eyes.

"Forgive Claudia. You said the words in the hospital, but you didn't mean them. You said them to console her. Now say them for yourself and mean them. You have to do that to move forward."

"Are you a psychologist, too?"

"Dime-store variety."

There was a long silence again.

"Forgive her," Alex finally said. "In your heart I know you already have. That's why you stayed by her bedside until she died."

He still didn't say anything.

"Say 'I forgive you, Mother.' Close that door forever. Feel those words, Brodie."

She waited for what seemed like an hour, but it was only seconds.

"I forgive you, Mother."

She waited again.

"I forgive you, Mother. I really do." He looked at her. "I really do."

She threw herself into his arms, kissing his face repeatedly.

When they came up for air, he asked, "Hungry?"

"Ravenous."

He swung his legs over the side of the bed and reached for his jeans. "I'll put Camila's enchiladas in the oven."

She tugged on his shirt and quickly followed.

In the kitchen, she could see that he was so much better. He actually smiled a couple of times and she knew he was going to be okay.

She slept another night in his bed and left early so she could make it to work on time. Buck's patience was wearing thin.

"THIS IS STARTING to be a pattern," Buck said as she entered the house.

She poured a cup of coffee. "Not for long. I rented an apartment yesterday."

He laid down the paper. "What'd you do that for?"

She blinked. "I told you I was moving out."

"I didn't think you meant it. And why do you need an apartment? You have a home right here."

"Are you getting senile? You've told me many times I needed to move out, get married, have kids, blah, blah, blah."

"Are you married?"

"No," she said slowly as if speaking to a child. "We've talked about this."

"Well, go, but you're not leaving Naddy with me."

She placed her hands on her hips. "We've had this discussion, too. You said you wouldn't kick Naddy out."

"I've changed my mind."

She saw that look in his eyes that she'd seen the other day—fear. He was afraid of losing his family. Could Buck actually love her and Naddy? Could he really have a heart?

"No. You don't get to do that." She headed for the stairs, knowing she wasn't changing her mind.

"It'll be on your head if I kill Naddy."

"I'll visit you in prison," she called, running up the stairs.

She always knew she didn't have a normal family, but now she wondered what defined normal. Was it a woman stealing a baby and pretending it was her own? Or was it, like Naddy, living life to the fullest? Or was it, like Buck, keeping all his emotions inside? Maybe it was living life the best way you could—accepting, forgiving and loving.

Chapter Sixteen

In the next few days Brodie knew he'd turned a corner. All because of Alex and her caring. She'd gotten him to open up and talk. He never had a problem talking, but lately he'd shut down his emotions, except with her.

He still wasn't sure about a lot of things, but he was ready to face each day—and the Braxton family. Once he opened that door he had to be prepared to walk through it and deal with Travis Braxton—the man he was. Or the man he was supposed to be.

He was still hesitant, but Colter and Tripp encouraged him to take the first step. And Alex agreed with them. So he made the phone call and arranged to visit on Sunday. He took Alex with him and he was beginning to see that she was his comfort blanket.

The day was overwhelming and at times he felt as if he was suffocating. Helen and Maggie smothered him with attention and George asked a million questions. His nephew, Cody, and his niece, Amber, were there, too. He made it through the meal but as soon as it was over, he had to get away—just to breathe.

Holding Alex that night made it all better. But how long could he continue to use her? He wanted to offer her a future, but he was still having a lot of conflicting emotions. How could he spend his life with her if he didn't know who he was?

Years ago, he'd learned once you fell off a horse, you dusted off your britches and got back on. So that's what he did. He went back to the Braxtons for shorter visits. George showed him his horses and they rode together.

The next weekend he taught Cody to rope and he cranked the tractor and mowed the weeds that covered the property. That constant knot in his stomach began to melt away as he got to know his new family.

Alex moved into an apartment and bought new furniture. He helped her arrange it, then he spent the night with her, "breaking in the bed" as she called it. The next morning he knew he couldn't live in the city. He was country, pure and simple, and he wondered at the difference in him and Alex. Was the gulf too wide to make a relationship work? Would she give up the city for him?

At the moment he didn't feel he had the right to ask that of her. But soon he'd have to make a decision about Alex. The thought of letting her go sent a pain through his chest. Love had finally bitten Brodie Hayes and he didn't have a clue what to do about it.

Under normal circumstances it would be very simple. Get married, have kids, be happy. Was that possible for them? Or was he just clinging to her out of need brought on by the shock of his real identity?

Why did life have to be this difficult? Riding a bull

was so much easier. Broken bones healed, but his heart was another matter.

ALEX WAS HAVING a headache of a day. It started with Naddy and Buck arguing over the reward money. Naddy had her sights set on a Cadillac. Just as she was trying to make Naddy see sense and keep Buck's temper in check, her phone rang.

Mike wanted to let her know that Ray Sims had leaked Brodie's story to the press for a price. Damn. She would need more than Tylenol to get through this day. She immediately called Brodie, then the Braxtons.

When the story broke, the news spread rapidly. Alex saw that it shook Brodie. He became quiet, almost distant, and for the first time she couldn't reach him. That scared her.

BY THE END OF THE WEEK Brodie knew he had to get away from all the rumors and gossip. He'd never thought so many people could be interested in his life. As much as he wanted to, he couldn't seek comfort or lean on Alex anymore.

It was time to get his life straight and to sort through everything he was feeling, especially about Alex. Going on like he was wasn't an option anymore. He had to find out who he really was. Until he figured that out he and Alex didn't have anything more than a sexual relationship.

For the first time in his life, he wanted more than that from a woman.

He told George and Helen because he felt they had

a right to know. Disappearing out of their lives without a word would only hurt them and he couldn't do that. They deserved his respect.

He was surprised by their reaction. They understood and asked that he call every now and then to let them know he was okay. He hugged them before he left and he didn't feel like he was coming apart at the seams. That was progress, but it didn't clear his head of all the confusion and the doubts.

Driving away, there was one thought on his mind. Now he had to tell Alex.

HER JEEP WAS AT the office so he knew she was at work. The apartment was too personal, too comfortable, and he'd rather talk to her here.

He opened the door to loud voices. A stout man with a crew cut came out of Alex's office. He looked mad enough to eat rusty nails.

"You're not buying it. That's all I have to say," he shouted over his shoulder.

The man stopped and glared at him. "What do you want?"

This man is as mean as some of the bulls I've ridden. This could only be Buck Donovan.

"I'm here to see Alex."

"Well, she's busy, so do whatever the hell you want." Saying that, he slammed shut his office door.

"Nice meeting you," he murmured, removing his hat and walking toward Alex's office. He could hear her voice clearly—that patient, tolerant voice he knew well.

"This is it, Naddy, and we're not arguing about it

anymore. No Cadillac. You can't afford it. Buck has agreed to let you have the hot tub."

"Hot damn. That's what I wanted all along. Who needs a big old Cadillac? My Buick drives just fine."

"Good, then…" Alex glanced up and saw him. "Brodie, come in."

"I can come back later."

"No need. This is my grandmother, Naddy. And Naddy, this is Brodie Hayes."

Naddy turned to him. "How do you do, handsome?"

"I do just fine, ma'am."

"Uh-huh." She eyed him up and down. "I bet you do."

Brodie saw where Alex got her sense of humor. This lady was like a lit firecracker. He had a feeling she went off regularly.

"Naddy, don't you have a hot tub dealer to see?"

"Oh…yeah. I do." She picked up a large bag from Alex's desk. "Tell you what, handsome. You can join Ethel and me in the hot tub anytime."

"Ah…" He was at a loss for words.

"Don't mind her," Alex said. "Her elevator doesn't go quite to the top some days."

"Uh-oh. I see now. My granddaughter has you staked out already." Naddy winked at him. "She has good taste. Got that from me, yes, she did."

"Naddy. Hot tub."

"I'm gone, honeychild."

Alex came around the desk and Brodie took a step backward. "Don't come any closer."

"Why? Are you contagious?"

"I can't say what I have to if you're within a foot of me."

Alex's stomach sank. "What is it?"

"I'm leaving for a while."

She licked her lips. "Leaving?"

"Yes. I need to get away to figure out who I am."

"Brodie, I'm sorry about the newspaper article."

"The article is only part of this whole mess."

"Brodie…"

He held up a hand. "Let me finish. I'll try to explain how I feel." He drew a deep breath. "It's as if I'm in the dark, balancing on a tight rope. I can either make it to the other side and daylight, or tumble into a never-ending darkness." He paused. "You've been my comfort blanket, there to help me through it all and holding you I can glimpse a sliver of light. But I'm still balancing precariously between Brodie Hayes and Travis Braxton. For my own peace of mind I can't keep using you to get through another day. You deserve better than that. I have to find out if I'm Brodie or Travis."

She told herself to be strong—to let him go without regrets. With dignity. But this would be the hardest thing she ever had to do. She swallowed the lump that formed in her throat. "How long will you be gone?"

"I'm not sure."

"What about your ranch?"

"Joey and his dad will look after it. Colter will check on them from time to time."

"Sounds as if you're not planning on coming back."

"I have a lot of thinking to do."

"Have you told the Braxtons?"

"Yes, and they were very supportive and understanding. The way parents are supposed to be, I guess."

"Then this is goodbye." Tears stung the back of her eyes but she stoically refused to cry. She wouldn't do that to him.

He looked into her eyes. "It isn't just a sexual thing between us. I've felt more for you than any woman I've ever known. Without you, I wouldn't have made it through the past three months. But somehow all those feelings are jumbled up with the pain and the heartache. I don't know what's real anymore. I have to go to get my head straight. Please understand that."

"I'm trying to."

"Take care of yourself."

She nodded, unable to speak.

He turned and walked out. Just like that her world came tumbling down around her, leaving her scarred and empty. She gulped in air so she could breathe, but the pain was still there. And probably always would be.

She took a chance and gave her heart to the cowboy. And the cowboy wasn't sure what he wanted. But she was. She'd wait forever if she had to because she knew exactly who he was.

The man she loved.

BRODIE JUST STARTED DRIVING, trying not to see that hurt look in Alex's eyes. He called Tripp to let him know he wouldn't be around for a while. Colter already knew. Both of them tried to talk him out of going, but he didn't change his mind.

He took Interstate 35 into Waco, then U.S. Highway 190 into Killeen, Texas, and on to the Fort Hood army base. There were many restricted areas so he parked his truck a safe distance away from the main gate and took in the scene. Men in uniform were everywhere; barracks, hangars, airfields and numerous buildings were in the distance. The real Brodie Hayes would have lived in a place like this, following in his father's footsteps.

But that wasn't him—the person Brodie was inside. He'd known that from an early age.

He drove on to Austin, then San Antonio. From there he took Interstate 10 into Houston. The heavy traffic made him wish he'd taken another route, but he didn't know where he was going. Anywhere was his destination. As he inched his way across Houston, he definitely knew this busy, hectic lifestyle wasn't for him, either.

It was dark when he stopped in Galveston so he checked into a motel. He was dead tired. He didn't even care about eating. The next morning he walked along the beach for hours, then sat in the sand staring out at the never-ending water. Inside he was balancing on the tightrope with all the strength he had.

He wasn't sure how long he stayed in Galveston. He found a measure of peace just watching the water. One day as he strolled along, he looked down to see his boots covered in sand. White gritty sand eating into the leather.

He was wearing his boots on the beach.

That spoke volumes to him. Who would wear boots on a beach? A cowboy. He was a cowboy. He already knew that, but it was suddenly clearer than ever. Mesmerized by the sand, he asked himself the same question he'd asked Colter and Tripp—how do you put a broken cowboy back together? They didn't have an answer and neither did he. Once he figured that out maybe everything would fall into place. Maybe he'd have a name for the cowboy.

He removed his hat and threw it into the air. It landed next to a couple of girls sunbathing. A blonde in a bikini picked it up and glanced toward him. She rose to her feet, all curvy and feminine. He had no reaction at all, other than to notice that she was beautiful.

"Hey there, cowboy." She smiled as she approached him. "Are you lost?" She handed him his hat.

He took it. "Yes, ma'am. I'm lost. Thanks." Setting his hat on his head, he strolled away. He was lost but he was finally finding his way back.

"Hey. Don't run off. I'll help you," the blonde called after him.

"No, thanks. I know where I'm going now."

In his room, he called the Braxtons. When Helen answered, he wasn't sure what to say so he said what was in his heart. "I just wanted to let you know that I'm okay."

"Oh, Brodie, thank you for calling. It helps to hear your voice."

Brodie swallowed. "Is George there?"

"He's out mowing grass and repairing fences. He wants the place to look nice for when you visit."

"Tell him I said hi."

"I will. He'll be sorry he missed you. Take care of yourself and call when you can."

Helen didn't ask when he was coming home or pressure him. He was grateful for that. He hung up and wanted to call Alex, just to hear her voice. No one called him *cowboy* like she did. The pretty blonde on the beach couldn't hold a candle to Alex and the way she made him feel. He was beginning to think that what he felt for Alex was as real as it could get.

In the next hour, he was on the road, still searching for that elusive answer. Was he Brodie or Travis?

He headed back to Houston, then took U.S. 290 to Brenham and Texas Highway 36 through Caldwell. His destination was very clear—Bramble, Texas. He wanted to see Tripp and talk to his friend.

Tripp and his family lived on the Lady Luck Ranch and Brodie drove there via a shortcut on the country back roads. He stopped as he saw a truck and trailer half parked in the road—the trailer was backed into a loading chute. Two riders, a man and a young boy, were trying to pen a bull.

He got out and watched as the man swung a rope over his head, trying to rope the bull. Every time the rope fell short of the bull's sawed-off horns, the bull, worked up and angry, would charge the horses.

"Do you need some help?" Brodie called.

The man and boy rode over. "We've been trying to load this bull for over an hour, but he's one mean sonofagun."

"Why are you penning him by himself? He'd be much calmer with cattle."

"Because he broke through my fence into Mr. Shafer's pasture. Now Mr. Shafer, he ain't too friendly or neighborly. He said if I didn't get my bull off his property today, he's going to shoot him. We tried herding him toward my ranch, but all he wants to do is fight. Mr. Shafer let us use this fenced-off pen and corral, but that's not working, either."

"Maybe I can help."

"Can you ride?" the man asked, spitting chewing tobacco onto the ground.

"A little."

"This is my grandson, Nathan. He's trying to help, but that bull is a whole lot of mean."

The boy looked to be about twelve—no match for the bull.

"Can I borrow your horse, Nathan?"

"Yes, sir." Nathan quickly slid from the saddle.

Brodie jumped over the barbed-wire fence and grabbed the reins. He adjusted the stirrups and swung into the saddle.

"I'm Nate Johnson," the man introduced himself.

"Nice to meet you, Mr. Johnson." He rode closer. "May I have your rope?"

"Sure. I'm guessing you can rope." Nate unlooped the rope from the saddle horn and handed it to him.

"A little." He adjusted the rope into a big loop, getting a feel of it and the horse beneath him. The brown mare responded well to his signals.

Sitting back in the saddle, he thought about a plan—the best way to pen the bull. He, Colter and Tripp had done this many times. But the three of them together knew exactly what to do and when. Brodie wasn't sure Mr. Johnson was going to be much help.

As he looked at the wood structure of the corral, he saw that it had two gates—one on each side. One gate was opened.

"Nathan," he said. "Open the other gate."

"But the bull will just run through it." Mr. Johnson made his opinion known.

"Trust me."

"Sure," Nate replied. "Nothin' I've tried has worked."

Nathan hurried to open the other gate.

"Nathan," Brodie called. "When I shout to close it, I want you to close it as fast as you can and get out of the way."

"Yes, sir. Wow! This is going to be like a rodeo."

Brodie smiled inwardly. He hoped everything went like he had it planned in his head, although usually a bull had a way of changing plans.

The bull was a Brahma mix, which wasn't good. They were known for their fiery temperament. In a corner of the pen, the bull pawed at the ground, snot running out of his nose, his eyes on the riders as if he was daring them to come after him.

"Okay, Mr. Johnson. See if you can get him out of that corner, so I can get the rope over his head."

"You're pretty sure you can rope him."

"I'll give it my best."

"Uh-huh." Nate rode toward the bull and Brodie stood in the stirrups, ready to throw the rope.

When the bull charged Nate, he spun his horse toward the middle of the pen and the bull followed. With one quick movement, Brodie swung the rope above his head and sailed it toward the bull. It fell in a circle over the bull's horns. He jerked the rope tight and looped the end over the saddle horn, backing up the horse to further tighten the rope.

Not liking the rope, the bull threw up his head and jerked from side to side, trying to dislodge it. Brodie turned his horse and yanked on the rope. The animal charged the horse and Brodie. He kneed the horse and they galloped at a run for the corral with the bull behind them.

Brodie flew through one gate, then the next. "Shut the gate," he shouted, and jumped from the horse, helping Nathan with the gate. The bull rammed into it and the boards weakened from the contact. Brodie quickly wrapped the rope around a large center post. The bull bashed it repeatedly with his head and Brodie tightened the rope. After butting it a few times, the animal settled down.

"Wow," Nathan said. "I've never seen anything like that."

Nate closed the other gate. "Mighty fine work."

Brodie crawled onto the fence. "I'd let him settle down a little bit before you load him."

"Oh, I'm not loadin' him." Mr. Johnson dismounted. "You roped him, you get to do the job."

Brodie tipped back his hat and smiled. The cowboy way—that's how Nate did things. And Brodie knew the rules well—once you start something, you finish it.

"You got it."

He loosened the rope enough to slip it off the horns. The bull threw up his head and began to run around the corral, looking for an escape. He charged into one corner, then another before he ran into the open chute. Brodie slammed the gate shut before the big animal realized he was in a trap.

Crawling atop the chute, he shouted and shouted until the bull loped into the trailer. Brodie was right behind him, locking the gate of the trailer. There was no more escape. The bull was ready to haul.

Brodie leaped to the ground. Nate stood waiting for him.

"I think you've done this a time or two before," Nate said, squinting at him. "Don't believe I caught your name."

He held out his hand. "Brodie Hayes," he replied without even thinking about it.

Nate pumped his hand vigorously. "Well, I'll be a sonofagun. I knew you weren't no ordinary cowboy. You're a three-time world champion. You could've of just ridden that bull into the pen."

"Oh, boy. Wow!" Nathan crawled between the barbed wires. "Wait a minute." He ran to the truck and came back with a magic marker. "Sign my T shirt, please." He turned his back to Brodie.

He scribbled *Brodie Hayes* in bold letters across Nathan's back. It all fell into place at that moment. That's who he was, a cowboy and a bull rider. He'd spent years learning the skill and his name mattered because it identified who he was and labeled all the hard work and sacrifice. And it labeled him. That's what had been so difficult, trying to let go of the man he was inside.

Now he knew he didn't have to do that. Whether he was Brodie Hayes or Travis Braxton he was still a cowboy, a bull rider. Once a cowboy, always a cowboy. He felt comfortable in Brodie Hayes's skin and he wasn't going to change that. Nothing could.

He walked away with a spring in his stride. As he got into his truck, he waved at the Johnsons and drove away.

How do you put a broken cowboy back together?

He now knew the answer to that question—with the love of a good woman.

Alex.

Chapter Seventeen

Alex soon discovered that life went on even when you had a broken heart. As each day passed and Brodie didn't call, her hopes grew dimmer and dimmer. So she threw herself into the Davis case, often working late. Going home to an empty apartment wasn't all that appealing.

She'd gotten used to Brodie filling it up. She'd gotten used to a lot of things about Brodie, especially his arms around her in the middle of the night. And she couldn't believe how much she missed him—how much a part of her he'd become.

But she was trying to go on. She'd met a neighbor, Denise, and it was nice to have a girlfriend to talk to again. She'd missed that after Patsy had moved away. Talking on the phone wasn't the same thing. Yet no matter how many friends she had to talk to, none of them could fill the void of Brodie.

As she hurried into the office, she heard loud voices coming from Buck's room. Was Naddy here again? She was getting tired of playing referee, although lately they'd been getting along better than usual.

Naddy had gotten her money and she wasn't trying to blow it all at once. She'd given some to Alex to put away for when she needed it. Naddy and Ethel had an Atlantic City trip planned for the end of the month. The hot tub had been installed and it kept Naddy and Ethel occupied—for now.

As she neared Buck's office, she could hear the voices clearly. It wasn't Naddy's.

"Just get the hell out of Dallas." That was Buck's grumpy voice.

"I'm sorry. I can't do that. I know I promised, but I have to see her." She didn't recognize the woman's voice.

"What the hell for? It's not going to make a bit of difference."

"For me it will."

"Stop thinking about yourself and think about what this will do to her."

Alex didn't have a clue what they were talking about so she started to just go to her office. But something propelled her forward.

"What's going on?" she asked.

Buck came around his desk. "Just go to your office. This doesn't concern you."

"Okay. But you don't have to be so grouchy."

"Are you Alex?" the woman asked.

She glanced from her father's set face to the woman's. She was pale, her skin almost chalklike, and her eyes were sunk in her head. She was painfully thin. Alex knew the woman was ill.

"Yes, I'm Alex. Do I know you?"

"No, you don't," Buck answered. "She was just leaving."

"I'm not leaving, Buck."

Buck took the woman's arm in a firm grip. "Yes, you are."

The woman jerked away and stumbled backward to a chair.

Alex ran to her aid. "Are you okay?"

"I just need a moment." She took several deep breaths.

"Go to your office, Alex. I'll handle this."

Alex glared at Buck. "Stop being so mean." She opened Buck's small refrigerator, got a bottle of water and handed it to the woman. "This might help."

"Thanks." The woman took several sips, staring at Alex. "You're so pretty. Just like I knew you'd be."

"Oh. You've seen me before?"

"No."

Alex was taken aback, not sure what to make of her answer. She thought it best to let Buck handle whatever was going on. Besides, the veins on his neck were popped out and he looked ready to explode. Naddy was usually the perpetrator of that effect.

"Just go," Buck said again and she turned to leave.

"I'm Gwen Canton," the woman said in a rush, breathing heavily. "I'm your…your mother."

Alex swung back. *"What!"*

"I'm your mother." Gwen said the words very clearly this time.

Alex waited for Buck to deny what the woman was saying, but he just stood there white as a sheet.

"You must be delusional," she said, trying to hold on

to a thread of sanity. "My mother's name was Joan." She looked at her father. "Buck?"

He walked to his chair and sank into it. Tiny frissons of fear shot through her heart. This couldn't be happening to her, not after what she'd been through with Brodie.

She wanted to rant and scream at Buck, but anger never accomplished anything. She'd learned that from Brodie. Now she just wanted answers.

"Tell me how you can be my mother."

Gwen stared at Buck, but he remained stone-faced.

Gwen clasped the bottle in her hands. "I worked at the police station when Buck was a cop. Joan had had three miscarriages and cried a lot because she desperately wanted a baby. The doctor told her it probably wasn't going to happen. Buck was upset and when he worked the nightshift he'd talk to me. One thing led to another and we had an affair."

Buck got up and walked to the window.

"When I found out I was pregnant, I didn't know what to do. My family is very strict Baptist and I was involved with a married man. I was young, unmarried and I didn't want the baby. I decided to give it up for adoption. But Buck wouldn't hear of it. He told Joan and though she was angry with him for his infidelity, she wanted his baby. I agreed to give the baby to them."

Gwen took a swallow of water. "I quit my job and moved to Austin. Buck paid for my apartment and all my medical bills. Joan told everyone she was pregnant again and wore maternity clothes. When I started having contractions, I called them and they came to Austin. As soon as I delivered you, the nurse carried you to Joan.

I never got to hold you. I was only told you were a girl."
She took a long breath. "Buck gave me ten thousand
dollars to start over again and I promised to never come
back or interfere in your life."

"But you are here," Alex said, surprised at how
calm she was.

"Yes." Gwen studied the bottle. "I went to nursing
school, got a good job and fell in love. My husband had
two children and I raised them. Sadly I was never able
to have any of my own again." She clasped the bottle
tighter. "I'm an emergency room nurse and one evening
a drug addict broke into our medicine cabinet. He
knocked out one nurse and I found him jamming a
needle into his arm. We struggled and he thrust the
needle into me before the security guards could contain
him. He was HIV positive."

Alex swallowed. "So you have AIDS?"

Gwen looked directly at her. "Yes. I don't have much
time left. I didn't come here lightly, but when you're facing
death you think about so many things especially all the sins
that you've committed over the years. I guess I'm looking
for redemption, forgiveness for what I did to you."

"For heaven sakes," Buck growled, but they didn't
pay him any attention.

Gwen set the bottle on the floor and reached for her
purse. She pulled out a slip of paper. "I've written the
name of the motel and room number where my
husband and I are staying. We'll be here for a couple
of days." Gwen stood and laid the paper on Buck's
desk. "Think about what I said. I hope we can talk
again." She left quietly.

Alex picked up the paper and stared at Buck. "You could have told me."

"Joan didn't want you to know and I…"

Suddenly Alex couldn't take anymore. She bolted for the door.

"Alex!" Buck shouted.

But she wasn't listening. She jumped into her Jeep and headed…she didn't know where she was going. Just away. Her pulse raced and tears stung her eyes so she pulled into a parking lot.

Brodie had said that she didn't understand how he was feeling. At the time she thought she did. But she wasn't even close. This kind of betrayal was debilitating and it could cripple her—if she let it.

She watched a stream of cars stopped at a red light. The light turned green and the cars moved on. This was a red light moment in her life, as Brodie's discovery had been for him.

She'd learned from him and what he'd been through. His love empowered her, made her stronger, and this red light wasn't going to change a thing. She wasn't sinking into self-pity, whining why, why, why. She had never known Joan so allowing herself a green light was easy. Buck was still her father. Naddy was still her crazy grandmother. Her life was still the same, except now she knew the truth.

It came home to her just how difficult this had been for Brodie—to deal with being another person. She didn't truly understand until now….

She realized she still had Gwen's paper clutched in her hand. Unfolding it, she knew she had to tell Gwen that there was nothing to forgive. She hadn't had a *Leave It To Beaver* life, but who did? She had Buck, who was always there for her even though she had a hard time understanding him. And she had Naddy, who made her laugh and taught her to accept people the way they were. Life wasn't all that bad.

Glancing at the name of the motel, she started the Jeep. As she pulled out into traffic, her cell rang. It was Mrs. Bigly, Buck's next-door neighbor.

"I'll be right there, Mrs. Bigly," she said.

What Mrs. Bigly had told her couldn't be true, but she had to find out. She whizzed through traffic and soon zipped into Buck's driveway. She noticed the grass was almost brown. Damn. Quickly, she turned on the sprinklers and ran into the house.

She marched through the den to stare out the French doors leading to the patio. Mrs. Bigly was right. Naddy and Ethel were in the hot tub naked as jaybirds. Good grief, the world didn't need to see this.

She swung open the door. "Naddy, what do you think you're doing?"

"Honeychild, get in the tub with us." Naddy was unperturbed by her appearance.

"Not for a million bucks. Get out this instant. The neighbors are complaining."

"That old Bigly lady, right?" Naddy took a swig from the beer can she had perched on the edge of the tub.

"She's younger than you."

"She's a busybody."

"Get out of the tub." Her voice rose.

"Bigly can't see a thing."

"Her patio is right next door."

"I can't see her, so how can she see us?"

"Have you got cataracts?"

"No. I have a Buick. You know that."

Alex heaved a put-out sigh. "I said cataracts, not Cadillac."

"Oh. Now I might have those."

"Get out of the tub."

"Okay. Keep your britches on." Naddy made to get up.

"No," Alex shrieked, seeing more than she needed to. "I'll get your robe and I'll get one for Ethel, too. Don't move until I get back."

"Make up your mind."

Alex hurried inside to Naddy's room and rummaged through the pile of clothes for a robe. She couldn't find one. The humor of the situation got to her and she sank to her knees laughing.

Suddenly the events of the day hit her like a brick wall and the laughter turned to tears. Loud sobs racked her body. She had a mother and she was dying. She was losing a mother—again.

Brodie, I need you. Come home.

"Honeychild, what is it?" Naddy asked from the doorway, dressed in her robe. Ethel stood behind her.

"I was looking for your robe," she replied inanely, pushing up to sit on the bed.

"I had it outside. If I'd known it was going to upset you this much, I would never have done it." Naddy sat beside her. "Ethel and me just wanted to see what it was like. Hell, we don't get too many thrills these days."

"I'm not crying about that." She brushed away tears. "But don't ever do that again."

"Okay. Okay." Naddy rubbed her arm. "What's the waterworks about?"

"Joan wasn't my mother."

"Sure she was."

"I'll fix some coffee," Ethel said and went into the kitchen.

"What are you talking about, Alex?"

"Joan wasn't my mother," she repeated.

"Now I might be getting senile, but I know Joan was pregnant with you. She'd had three miscarriages and she was so happy to be able to get pregnant again. She and Buck went to Austin for a weekend and she started having contractions. You were born there and they brought you home in a couple of days."

Alex told Naddy the story she'd heard from Gwen.

"Buck had an affair!"

"Yes."

"That sly dog." Naddy rubbed her arm again. "Are you okay, child?"

"I'm trying…" She looked up to see her father standing in the doorway.

Naddy got up and shook her finger in Buck's face. "You lying dog. You tell her the truth and don't leave out anything. I ought to box your ears."

"Give it a rest, Naddy," Buck said. "This is the pot calling the kettle black."

"I know I'm not a saint."

"Well, neither am I."

"You got that one right, Bucky."

Buck shook his head. "Go somewhere else. I need to talk to Alex."

Naddy stomped out and Buck looked around. "This is a pigsty. Let's go to the kitchen."

Alex followed and noticed that Naddy and Ethel were back in the tub with their swimsuits on.

Buck poured a cup of coffee and sat down. "What do you want to know?"

Getting Buck to talk about personal things was a major accomplishment, so she pulled out a chair, ready to get her pound of flesh.

"Did you love Gwen?"

"No. I loved Joan, but she got very hard to live with. She was always depressed and crying. Each miscarriage made life that much harder."

"She forgave you for the affair?"

"After a lot of tears, yes. Once she knew Gwen didn't want the baby, that changed everything. The first moment she held you, she became a different person. She became the woman I married—happy, loving and caring. She adored you. She just wasn't given enough time."

"Why did you keep it a secret?"

Buck fingered his cup. "That's the way Joan wanted it. She wanted you to be our baby completely, and I'd hurt her so badly that I was willing to do anything she wanted."

"After her death, why didn't you tell me the truth?"

"You were two years old. What would you have understood? To me, you were Joan's daughter."

"But I wasn't."

"What does it matter who gave you life? Joan gave you her love. You were our kid."

She thought of Brodie. Helen had given him life, but his first loyalty had been to Claudia. A biological bond was one thing. But there was another kind of bond that was just as strong. It was called love.

Had Brodie already figured that out? Now he had to face the biological bond and make sense of it all. As did she.

The sudden revelation in her life seemed minor compared to what Brodie was going through. That first day when Helen had told her about her son, Alex had looked at Brodie's photo and felt a connection like she'd never felt before. Maybe subconsciously she had known they were kindred spirits. And eventually would become so much more. But now...

Now she had to deal with her father. "Yeah. I'm your kid. Can't escape that one."

"No, 'fraid not."

She scooted her chair forward. "When I asked about Joan, you would never talk much about her. Does Gwen have anything to do with that?"

"Oh, God." He got up for another cup of coffee. "You want your pound of flesh, don't you?"

"Every ounce."

He sat down again, staring into his cup. "I... ah...you know."

"You loved Joan?"

"Yeah. Talking about her wasn't easy because, well, you know."

"It hurt like hell."

"Yeah."

She stood. "Buck, you're too old for me to finish your sentences."

"Girl, that ain't me."

"It can be." She watched him for a moment. "How do you feel about me?"

"What?" He glanced up with a puzzled frown. "Well, you know."

"No, I don't. You have to say the words, Buck. I deserve that."

"You may not be Joan's daughter, but you sure act like her. She was on and on about that, too."

"How do you feel about me?"

He stared at her as if she'd suddenly grown two heads. "I…ah…love you."

She threw her arms around his neck and kissed his rough cheek. "I love you, too."

"Ah, girl, don't start that." He tried to push her away, but not very strongly. "We're not that kind of family."

"Things are changing at the Donovan house."

"You don't live here anymore," he reminded her. "And when are you gettin' all that stuff out of your old room? I could rent it out."

Normally those words would be hurtful to her, but not today. She'd heard the magic words.

She leaned in with her palms flat on the table. "Okay. Here's the deal. I'll forgive you if you'll forgive Naddy for your rotten childhood."

"That's two entirely different things. And it's blackmail."

"I learned from a pro."

Buck just stared into his cup.

"Forgive her so you can move on. It's time."

"I'll try."

She threw her arms around his neck again.

"Now let's don't start doing a lot of that," he grumbled.

A chuckle left her throat. "Get used to it." She walked to the door.

"Where you going?"

"I have a mother to see."

"Oh. I'm…you know."

"Sorry."

"Yeah."

"Got it." She ran to her Jeep, feeling the world opening up like it never had before. All she needed was for one hurt cowboy to come home.

Brodie, where are you?

Chapter Eighteen

Alex spent over an hour with Gwen. She didn't seem to want to know every detail of Alex's life, but asked if Alex was happy. She could honestly say she'd always been a happy person. With Naddy for a grandmother she had a built-in sense of humor.

Looking back she saw that the tension between Naddy and Buck made her stronger. It had taught her how to deal with people, to be diplomatic. It wasn't the Cleaver household, but it was her life.

Gwen wanted to know if she was married and she found herself talking about Brodie. She couldn't believe how natural it was to talk to her. But in the end they were strangers. They didn't have the time to build any kind of relationship. Again, Alex felt a sense of loss.

Gwen's husband had gone to the coffee shop to give them time alone and it was nice talking to the woman who had given her life.

As Gwen grew tired, Alex stood. "There's nothing for me to forgive. I'm sure you did the best you could at the time."

"Yes. I was young and scared, but there wasn't a day that I didn't think about you. When you're young, you think you can put it out of your mind. It's not that easy, though. I knew for me to die in peace I had to see you. I know that's selfish, but I..."

"It's okay," Alex told her.

"I sense that you're a very strong person."

"I'm very soft-hearted, though."

Gwen's pallid face cracked into a semblance of a smile. "Me, too. I get so involved in other people's problems."

"I guess I got that from you, then."

"Probably, but you're much stronger than I ever was. You get your strength from Buck."

"I have to be strong to put up with him."

"You have a wonderful sense of humor and you're an absolute delight. Thank you for being so understanding."

"After Brodie's turmoil, I could do no less."

"I wish I could meet him."

There was an awkward pause.

Gwen picked up a folder from the bed. "I wanted to give you this."

"What is it?"

"It's my medical history. There's also information about my parents and what I know of my grandparents."

"Oh."

"As a nurse, I know this will be important to you in the years ahead. You should know what's in your background."

"Thank you."

They hugged and said goodbye—the final goodbye.

For Alex knew she would never see her mother again. At least not alive. Tears burned her eyes as she drove away.

She couldn't go home—the apartment was too empty. So she headed for the Cowboy Up Ranch. Stopping at a convenience store, she bought some food just in case the dogs were hungry.

Everything was in darkness except for the spotlights around the barns. She grabbed the bag and got out. The dogs loped toward her and she reached into the bag for a hot dog. The store didn't have a wide selection of dog food and she wasn't sure what the dogs would eat, so she bought a dozen wieners.

The dogs gobbled them up and she wondered how often they were being fed. Replete, the dogs lay at her feet. She leaned back, breathed in the fresh air and enjoyed the peace and quiet of the ranch she was beginning to love.

Most people with any common sense wouldn't sit in the sweltering heat in the darkness by themselves. But her family wasn't strong on common sense.

Crickets chirped and a coyote howled in the distance. The wind ruffled the tree branches with an eerie sound. She decided common sense had been left out of her gene pool completely.

She stared through the darkness toward the road. Alex didn't know how long she sat there waiting, dreaming and hoping.

One of the dogs whined.

"I miss him, too."

BRODIE SAT OUTSIDE Alex's apartment waiting. Where was she? It was getting late. He tried her cell, but she didn't answer. He didn't leave a message because he wanted to see and talk to her in person. At midnight he gave up and went home. Evidently Alex was working a case or out of town.

He'd check with her father in the morning. Going home wasn't easy, but come hell or high water, he was seeing her tomorrow.

ALEX FELL ASLEEP. When she woke up, it was almost twelve. Damn. She had to get home. They were finishing up the Davis case and she wanted to be in early. She hurried to her apartment to catch a few more hours of sleep.

AS BRODIE CROSSED his cattle guard, he knew he was home. This was his land, his cattle and his house. Brodie Hayes lived here. All the doubts and confusion had disappeared.

George and Helen hadn't asked him to change his name and for that he was glad. He'd have to talk to them about what they expected from him, then he'd tell them what he could live with. Simple.

It should have been from the start, but his emotions had been running high and his thought process hadn't been too clear. The Braxtons were good people and he was now ready to form a relationship with them. Not a forced one, but a real one.

He crawled into bed dead tired. *Alex, where are you?* was his last thought.

WHEN HE AWOKE, it was almost noon. Dammit. He leaped from the bed and quickly showered and dressed. The last couple of weeks he hadn't slept well at all and it had caught up with him. In fifteen minutes, he was charging out the back door.

Two trucks pulled into his driveway. Colter and Tripp. For the first time he wasn't glad to see them. He wanted to get to Alex.

Tripp spotted him first. "Hey, you're home."

"I got back late last night."

They embraced.

"You're looking a hell of a lot better," Colter said.

"I am better. I know who I am."

Colter and Tripp glanced at each other. "Brodie Hayes," they shouted in unison.

"Yeah. I discovered that I'm a cowboy and a bull rider and it doesn't really matter what my name is. I know who the man is inside, but I'm comfortable in Brodie's skin. I still have to talk to George and Helen."

"It'll work out," Tripp told him.

"I know that now." He squinted at the noonday sun. "What are you guys doing here?"

"We baled that coastal in your lower bottom a couple of days ago," Colter said.

"And we decided to get the hay off the field today." Tripp slapped him on the back. "Now you can help."

"Ah...thanks, but could we do this another day?"

"Why?" Tripp asked. "We're here. Let's get it done."

"Not today."

Tripp and Colter glanced at each other again. "Oh." Tripp nodded.

Colter tipped his hat back. "I think he's found a way to put the broken cowboy back together."

"You bet." Brodie grinned. "Thanks. I'll get the hay off the field later."

"Nah," Tripp said. "We started it, we'll finish it."

"Thanks, guys. Gotta run."

"Tell Alex hi for us," Colter shouted.

Brodie jumped into his truck and smiled all the way to the cattle guard.

Driving into Dallas, he felt the anticipation building in him and he couldn't wait to see her. He wanted their meeting to be special and he wanted them to be alone. Stopping not far from her office, he thought about a plan. His hand hit the steering wheel. Oh yeah, he knew what he was going to do.

ALEX HEARD Buck shouting from her office and she hurried to see what was happening.

"Danny Davis's lawyer just called—he got a new trial for him. Hot damn, you did great work on this case."

"So did you."

"We make a damn good team."

"We're father and daughter."

"Yeah." Buck closed a file. "I'm proud of the way you handled the Gwen thing. You've really grown up."

She blinked, wondering if she'd heard him correctly. But she knew she had. It was just an old reflex reaction. Her father was now seeing her as adult.

"Thank you. I was there with Brodie when he went through the pain and disillusionment. Helping him helped me to deal with my mother's sudden appearance.

Gwen and I had a good talk yesterday and I'm fine with the whole situation."

"You sure about that?"

"Yeah. Gwen and her husband are leaving for Lubbock this morning. I feel a bit sad that I'll never get to know her. But she's very ill and I know she doesn't want me to remember her like that, so we said goodbye."

"I'm sorry," he said.

Her eyes opened wide. "You said that without any prompting."

"Mmm. I must be changing, too."

"Yeah." And it was a very good thing.

"You still seeing the cowboy?"

She sank into a chair and told her father about her feelings for Brodie. She ended by saying, "I don't think he's ever coming back."

"He will."

She wasn't so sure, but it was an incredible feeling talking to her father about something personal. Pushing to her feet, she said, "I better get back to work."

"Mrs. Davis is coming in this afternoon with a big check. After I deposit it, Connie and I are heading to the coast for a week."

She lifted an eyebrow. "So I'm old enough to know that you have a lady friend?"

He looked up. "Yep."

"Have you told Naddy you're leaving?"

"Not yet."

"But you will?"

Buck leaned back, the chair squeaking from the

pressure. "Yep. I'll tell her and she can even have Ethel stay with her while I'm gone. How's that?"

She made a circle with her thumb and forefinger. "Perfect."

As she walked out, she heard his chuckle.

She cleared off her desk and wondered what she was going to do for the next week. Her room at Buck's needed cleaning, so she could finish that chore while checking on Naddy. She plopped into her chair. She felt at loose ends without knowing how Brodie was doing. Or if he was coming back.

A man walked into her office. "Alex Donovan?"

"Yes."

He handed her an envelope and walked out.

Ripping it open, she quickly scanned the sheet of paper. One line was written on it: If you want to drive my big old truck, you know where to find me.

Brodie.

She ran to her Jeep. *He was back. He was back.* She should go home and change and do her hair and... Through all the thoughts, the Jeep kept steadily going toward Mesquite and the Cowboy Up Ranch.

Removing her clip, she ran her fingers through her hair and shook it out. She dug in her purse for lipstick and the car honked behind her. Damn! She had to keep the Jeep in her lane.

As she drove over the cattle guard and down the road, she saw his truck. He was definitely back. She braked to a stop and jumped out, her heart knocking against her ribs.

Brodie stepped out of the door and walked toward

her. He looked the same as the first day she'd seen him in boots, tight jeans and a cowboy hat. He was one handsome cowboy, but there was something different about him. There was a spring in his step and his eyes…the bluest eyes in Texas were free of pain.

"Hi there, cowboy."

"Hi." He grinned, showing off that gorgeous dimple.

"You going to let me drive your truck?"

"Anytime, anywhere. You can do whatever you want with it."

"Really?"

"Yes. Just like my heart, my body and my soul. They're yours."

She threw herself at him then and he caught her, swinging her around. Their lips met in an explosive kiss that went on and on. She knocked off his hat, caressing his hair, his face, his neck and his shoulders.

"I missed you," she breathed between to-die-for kisses.

"I missed you, too." He swung her into his arms and strolled into the house. The dogs barked behind them.

In the kitchen, he set her on her feet and she stood with her mouth open. Red roses were on the table, the cabinet and the coffee table. Lit candles were everywhere, burning warmly. An ice bucket with a bottle of champagne nestled in it caught her eye.

Brodie poured two glasses of champagne and handed her one. He cleared his throat and stared into her eyes. "Alex Donovan, I love you. Will you marry me?"

"Yes," she breathed, her voice shaky. Suddenly she was back in his arms being thoroughly kissed. She leaned her forehead against his. "You better hold me tight because I'm about to melt into a puddle on your floor."

"Then let's continue this elsewhere." He took her glass and she didn't realize she was still holding it. Together they walked into the bedroom.

There were more flowers and more candles. "I never knew you were so romantic."

"There's a lot you don't know about me."

She rubbed her finger along his lower lip, removing some of her lipstick. "I know what's important."

"Mmm." He slowly removed her blouse and lavished her breasts with sweet, warm kisses. She gave herself up to this man who she was going to love forever.

A LONG TIME LATER she lay cradled in his arms. He pushed up against the headboard and she sat beside him. He told her what had happened since he'd left.

"So you know who you are?"

"Yeah. I called George and Helen and told them. They just want me to be happy."

"And are you?"

"Finally, yes." He smiled and she leaned over to kiss his dimple.

"I've been thinking about having Braxton added to my name. It doesn't matter to me, but it would please George and Helen."

"You really have dealt with all this."

"Yes. I respond to Brodie Hayes, so I've decided to change my name to Brodie Braxton Hayes. What do you think?"

"I love it." She stroked his leg.

"And I really respond to that."

She giggled as he pulled her into his arms and kissed her deeply. "Wait. I have to tell you something."

He stopped his perusal of her mouth to look into her eyes. "What?"

She told him about her mother.

"Oh my God! And I wasn't here when you needed me."

"But you were with me in spirit. After trying to help you cope, I knew anger and bitterness would only cause more pain. I was actually very calm and in control. That is after I cried my eyes out."

"Oh, honey. I'm so sorry." He kissed the side of her face. "Strange though. After meeting Buck, it would seem more likely that you weren't his daughter."

"It's not about biology sometimes. It's about family—a family is usually what you make it."

"You're right. I thought my problems with Tom and Claudia grew out of us being so different, but they didn't. My problems grew out of my anger. I see that now. I don't want you to feel that kind of anger." He caressed her arm.

"I don't, believe me, and if you keep stroking me like that I'm going to start humming."

"I love you, and from this day forward I will be here for you forever."

"You better, cowboy."

He nuzzled her neck. "Where would you like to live after we get married?"

She drew back. "The Cowboy Up Ranch, of course."

"That was easy."

"I love it out here. I came last night and fed the dogs."

He frowned. "You're kidding."

"No. Why?"

"I was at your apartment waiting for you until midnight."

She burst out laughing. "We're two of a kind."

"Soul mates." He kissed her shoulder. "Never knew what the words meant until now."

She swung her feet off the bed and grabbed her jeans.

He sat up. "What are you doing?"

"I'm going to drive your big old truck."

"Alex."

She ran down the hallway laughing, feeling young, happy and so much in love. Happily ever after was loving a cowboy with the bluest eyes in Texas.

Epilogue

One year later

Brodie Braxton Hayes had turned forty-one and the party at the Cowboy Up Ranch was in full swing. Family and friends spilled from the wood deck to the yard, laughing, talking, waiting for the barbecue simmering on a pit.

Brodie stood with Tripp and Colter talking about horses, cattle and ranching. Morris, the Danielses' butler, and Tulley, the man who raised Colter, tended to the barbecue.

Naddy, Buck, Maggie and her husband, Steve, played poker on a card table. The kids played in the yard, trying to rope a lawn chair. Walker, Tripp and Camila's son, was walking now and he didn't like being left out. He managed to always get in the way. Jilly lugged him to Camila, but Walker always made his way back.

His parents sat talking to Griffin and Leona, Tripp's parents. His closest friends and family were all here, sharing his birthday. The only person missing was Cleo. She'd married Melvin and they'd moved to Austin to be near Melvin's daughter. He talked to her every now and then to make sure she was okay. She would always be his aunt.

Alex, Marisa and Camila were on the patio, sipping tea and talking. He was sure it was about babies. A year had made such a difference. It was filled with happiness and any lingering pain they got through together.

Gwen passed away and they went to Lubbock for the funeral. Buck went, too. Alex now had a better relationship with her father because the truth had been revealed. And Brodie also had a good relationship with his parents. It hadn't come easy, but he went the extra mile trying to ease their pain.

He'd legally added Braxton as his middle name. He didn't have to do that, but for them, he did. The past forty years were gone and he couldn't change that, but he could give them the rest of his life.

"Ellie, are you going to ride in the Founder's Day Parade in Bramble?" Jilly asked.

"Yes. Daddy said I could and Mommy bought me a new outfit."

"Great. Mama made mine and it's totally cool. We get to carry the flags and lead the parade."

"Wow!"

"And Cody and Amber are riding, too."

They were all becoming very good friends.

Jack, Colter and Marisa's four-year-old son, looked up at Colter. "Daddy, can I ride, too?"

"Sure, son," Colter replied.

"By myself?"

Colter picked up his son. As if sensing what Colter was going to say, Jack whispered, "Don't ask Mommy."

Because of what happened with Ellie, Marisa tended to be overprotective of her children. That was the biggest problem that Marisa and Colter had, but they had a way of working it out.

"Now, son…"

"What is it?" Marisa called, knowing something was amiss. She made her way to them.

"Jack wants to ride in the parade by himself."

"Oh."

"Mommy, please. I'm big."

"Okay. As long as you ride next to your daddy."

Jack bobbed his head up and down.

They all laughed and Jack went into Marisa's arms and she held him extra tight.

"I'll watch him, too, Mommy," Ellie promised.

"Thank you, baby."

Walker stomped on Tripp's boots and he swung him up in his arms. "Son, you're scratching some mighty fine Kincaid boots."

"Bring him to me," Leona said. "I'll hold him."

"No. I'll hold him," Griffin said.

"That's okay, Mom, Dad," Tripp replied. "I got him."

If Tripp and Camila had any problems, it was balancing a very large family without anyone getting their feelings hurt.

Camila and Alex came across the yard. "Mama, Mama," Walker shouted, wiggling down. Then he was off.

Camila caught him and kissed his cheek. "Sissy." Walker pointed to Jilly and he was off again. He knew how to dole out his affection.

Alex walked into his arms and he pulled her into his side, kissing her for a long moment.

"Happy birthday," she whispered, tightening her arm around his waist. "It's nice having everyone together."

"Mmm." Life was better than it had ever been all because of Alex and her love.

They all heard it at the same time—a baby wail from the mobile monitor Alex held in her hand. She made a sprint for the house, but Brodie overtook her. Helen was at the door, but she let them pass.

Brodie stared into the bassinet in the living room at their two-month-old son. "Hey, there, buddy. Did you wake up?" He carefully lifted him into his arms, but his son wanted something he couldn't give him—milk.

Alex took the baby from him, sat down and opened her blouse. He latched onto to a nipple greedily. Brodie watched in amazement. Just looking at them he knew his world had been completed in a way he'd never even dreamed. He could never dream this good.

Alex laid the baby on her shoulder to burp him, patting his back.

Helen poked her head in. "Is he awake?"

"Yeah," Brodie said. "Come on in."

George followed Helen into the room and they stared at the black-haired, blue-eyed baby. "May I hold him, please?" Helen asked in a hesitant voice.

"Sure," Alex replied and handed the baby to Brodie. He took his son to his mother, placing him in her arms. Helen cradled the baby to her. "I'm almost afraid to say his name."

"Don't be," Brodie told her, tickling the baby's cheek while laying the silver rattle next to him. "Say hi to your grandmother, Travis Braxton Hayes."

Travis flashed his dimple and tears rolled from Helen's eyes.

"Let me have him," George said, his voice shaky. "You're getting him all wet."

The kids began to edge into the room, followed by the grown-ups, waiting to look at the new baby.

Over the top of everyone's heads his eyes caught Alex's. "I love you," he mouthed.

She smiled and everything in his world was right. She made it that way by just being in his life. With her love, the broken cowboy had healed completely.

* * * * *

Happily ever after is just the beginning...

Turn the page for a sneak preview of
A HEARTBEAT AWAY
by
Eleanor Jones

Harlequin Everlasting—Every great love
has a story to tell. ™
A brand-new series from Harlequin Books

Special? A prickle ran down my neck and my heart started to beat in my ears. Was today really special?

"Tuck in," he ordered.

I turned my attention to the feast that he had spread out on the ground. Thick, home-cooked-ham sandwiches, sausage rolls fresh from the oven and a huge variety of mouthwatering scones and pastries. Hunger pangs took over, and I closed my eyes and bit into soft homemade bread.

When we were finally finished, I lay back against the bluebells with a groan, clutching my stomach.

Daniel laughed. "Your eyes are bigger than your stomach," he told me.

I leaned across to deliver a punch to his arm, but he rolled away, and when my fist met fresh air I collapsed in a fit of giggles before relaxing on my back and staring up into the flawless blue sky. We lay like that for quite a while, Daniel and I, side by side in companionable silence, until he stretched out his hand in an arc that encompassed the whole area.

"Don't you think that this is the most beautiful place in the entire world?"

His voice held a passion that echoed my own feelings, and I rose onto my elbow and picked a buttercup to hide the emotion that clogged my throat.

"Roll over onto your back," I urged, prodding him with my forefinger. He obliged with a broad grin, and I reached across to place the yellow flower beneath his chin.

"Now, let us see if you like butter."

When a yellow light shone on the tanned skin below his jaw, I laughed.

"There…you do."

For an instant our eyes met, and I had the strangest sense that I was drowning in those honey-brown depths. The scent of bluebells engulfed me. A roaring filled my ears, and then, unexpectedly, in one smooth movement Daniel rolled me onto my back and plucked a buttercup of his own.

"And do *you* like butter, Lucy McTavish?" he asked. When he placed the flower against my skin, time stood still.

His long lean body was suspended over mine, pinning me against the grass. Daniel…dear, comfortable, familiar Daniel was suddenly bringing out in me the strangest sensations.

"Do you, Lucy McTavish?" he asked again, his voice low and vibrant.

My eyes flickered toward his, the whisper of a sigh escaped my lips and although a strange lethargy had crept into my limbs, I somehow felt as if all my nerve endings were on fire. He felt it, too—I could see it in his warm brown eyes. And when he lowered his face to mine, it seemed to me the most natural thing in the world.

None of the kisses I had ever experienced could have even begun to prepare me for the feel of Daniel's lips on mine. My entire body floated on a tide of ecstasy that shut out everything but his soft, warm mouth, and I knew that this was what I had been waiting for the whole of my life.

"Oh, Lucy." He pulled away to look into my eyes. "Why haven't we done this before?"

Holding his gaze, I gently touched his cheek, then I curled my fingers through the short thick hair at the base of his skull, overwhelmed by the longing to drown again in the sensations that flooded our bodies. And when his long tanned fingers crept across my tingling skin, I knew I could deny him nothing.

* * * * *

*Be sure to look for A HEARTBEAT AWAY,
available February 27, 2007.
And look, too, for THE DEPTH OF LOVE
by Margot Early, the story of a couple
who must learn that love comes in many guises—
and in the end it's the only thing that counts.*

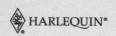

HARLEQUIN®

E V E R L A S T I N G L O V E™

Every great love has a story to tell™

Save $1.⁰⁰ off

the purchase of
any Harlequin
Everlasting Love novel

Coupon valid from January 1, 2007
until April 30, 2007.

Valid at retail outlets in the U.S. only.
Limit one coupon per customer.

5 65373 00076 2   (8100) 0 11302

HEUSCPN0407

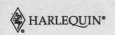

REQUEST YOUR FREE BOOKS!
2 FREE NOVELS PLUS 2
FREE GIFTS!

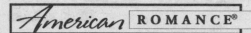

Heart, Home & Happiness!

HAR07

This February...

Catch NASCAR Superstar *Carl Edwards* in
SPEED DATING!

Kendall assesses risk for a living—so she's the last person you'd expect to see on the arm of a race-car driver who thrives on the unpredictable. But when a bizarre turn of events—and NASCAR hotshot Dylan Hargreave—inspire her to trade in her ever-so-structured existence for "life in the fast lane" she starts to feel she might be on to something!

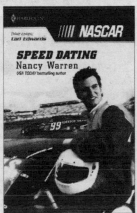

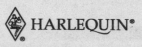

HARLEQUIN®

American **ROMANCE**®

COMING NEXT MONTH

#1153 HER SECRET SONS by Tina Leonard
The Tulips Saloon
Pepper Forrester has a secret—make that two secrets. Thirteen years ago she became pregnant with Luke McGarrett's twin boys and, knowing him as she did, didn't tell him he was a father. With both of them living in Tulips again, the time has come to confess. All looks to be well, until history begins to repeat itself....

#1154 AN HONORABLE MAN by Kara Lennox
Firehouse 59
Priscilla Garner doesn't want a man, nor does she need one. She's more interested in being accepted as the only female firefighter at Station 59. But when she needs a date—platonic, of course—for her cousin's wedding, she turns to one-time fling Roark Epperson. He knows she's not looking for long-term, but that doesn't mean he isn't planning on changing her mind!

#1155 SOMEWHERE DOWN IN TEXAS by Ann DeFee
Marci Hamilton loves her hometown of Port Serenity, but life's been a little dull lately. So she enters a barbecue sauce cook-off with events held all over Texas. Although it's sponsored by country music superstar J. W. Watson, Marci wouldn't recognize him—or any singer other than Willie Nelson. So when a handsome cowboy comes to her aid, she has no idea it's J.W. himself....

#1156 A SMALL-TOWN GIRL by Shelley Galloway
Still stung from her former partner's rejection, Genevieve Slate joins the police department in sleepy Lane's End hoping for a fresh start and a slower pace of life. But a sexy math teacher named Cary Hudson, a couple of crazed beagles and a town beset by basketball fever mean there's no rest in store for this small-town cop!

www.eHarlequin.com

HARCNM0207